Superficial

ANNA KILMER SKINNER

For Sonja, Sarah, and Aliana, three amazing young women whose love and happiness make every difficult day fade away into the backdrop of a life that is truly wonderful after all.

Special thanks to Jane Isenberg, Beth Kilmer, Hugh Kilmer, Brian Skinner, Sonja Skinner, Sarah Skinner, and Aliana Kilmer-Setrakian for your generous support and guidance. I couldn't have done it without you!

SUMMER 2003

PROLOGUE

"What's wrong?" Violet asks, noticing her friend's eyes on her.

"This show is so dumb," Tonya sighs loudly from her corner of the black leather couch.

"I like Goosebumps," Violet protests. "I'm not scared of it, but I still like it." It's a lazy summer Saturday morning, and Violet is curled up on the couch at her best friend's house. They start third grade in three weeks.

"Goosebumps is okay, but I'm bored." Violet's companion scratches carelessly at a worn patch on the arm of the sofa as if to emphasize her point.

"C'mon, Tonya, I never get to watch t.v."

"I know. Your mom is weird. Let's go watch in my mom and dad's room, at least." Tonya slides off the couch and leads the way out of the massive living room, down a wide hall and up a staircase to her parents' room.

The girls climb onto the king sized bed, using arms and legs to make their way onto the tall mattress. Tonya grabs the remote from the bedside table, turns the t.v. on, and seems to have a thought. She tosses the remote to Violet and leans way over to reach into the drawer under the lamp.

Violet turns the t.v. to Goosebumps, but her attention is on Tonya. "Watcha doin'?"

"Shhh," Tonya scolds, even though they're alone in the house. Tonya's mom is next door having coffee with a neighbor. "Wait 'til you see this," she smiles conspiratorially.

"What is it?" Violet scoots closer, remote in hand.

Tonya strains to pull a shoebox out of the drawer without falling off the bed. She puts it on the bed between herself and Violet, then reaches back into the drawer and pulls a notebook out. Violet looks at the box, feeling increasingly nervous. She considers that she ought to say something, but curiosity wins out. Tonya sets the notebook in her lap and nods toward Violet. "Open the box," she grins.

Violet's nervous, but she can't let her friend down. She's not in kindergarten, after all. She pulls off the lid. "Oh my gosh!" she laughs self consciously. She can see two candles, a lighter, a set of leopard fur handcuffs, and at least one glossy magazine underneath it all.

"Look at the magazines," Tonya urges.

"What's in the notebook?" Violet asks, hoping to avoid becoming any more uncomfortable than she already is.

"Check this out," the little girl dares as she opens the notebook. There's writing on the lined pages, but it's obscured by a folded piece of printer paper. "Ooh, something new!" Tonya opens the paper to a photo of her mother, naked, with her arms around a man who is not Tonya's father.

Violet watches Tonya's face fall, clearly not expecting this. "Tonya…"

"Shut-up," Tonya corrects her friend, and everything goes back into the drawer as if this had never happened.

FALL 2011

1

Everything is fine when Violet first gets to Tonya's. They're messing around on Facebook, and of course Tonya has a million people chatting her. Tonya's pretty, but from the number of guys she has after her all the time, you would think she was some kind of supermodel. She's petite all the way around and looks likes she was made for those Hollister and Abercombie clothes she always wears. She has long, straight, dirty blonde hair, a cute little nose, and perfect skin.

Violet first starts getting annoyed when Tonya disses Teah. "Holy shit, look what Teah just posted," Tonya laughs, pointing to a picture of Teah in her bathing suit. "What is she thinking? She looks like crap."

"So how come you just posted that?" asks Violet, pointing to Tonya's written comment: YOU'RE SO BEAUTIFUL!!! "I mean, if you really think she looks bad, just don't say anything. I think she looks pretty good. I wish I looked like that in a bikini."

"Whatever, you post comments like that all the time. I mean, you told Cecilia she looked great with her new haircut, and we both know she looked like crap. So what should we do Friday?" Tonya keeps typing.

At this point, Violet isn't real interested in making plans with Tonya. *I told Cecilia she looked great because she asked what we thought, and I wasn't gonna make her feel bad. She couldn't change her haircut anyway, and I **told** her I liked it* *better the other way.* "I don't know. I need to find out what Desmond is doing." *And I probably don't want to hang out with you anyway.*

"Oh right, can't spend a Friday night without Desmond! I was thinking of having some people over, but just single people. Like Laura, Marcus, Jamal, Amanda, Tim... I'm so sick of everyone being all into their lovers. I just wanna hang out and have fun. I might invite Evan over too."

Now Tonya is really pushing Violet's buttons. *Wow, God forbid I should wanna hang out with somebody besides you, Your Highness. You know I probably won't get to see Desmond all week. And what do you mean, 'invite Evan too'?* "Isn't Evan going out with Teah?"

"Yeah, but he's really not that into her. I don't even know why they're together. He's cute, isn't he?" As an extremely popular and attractive 17-year-old girl, Tonya has the power to make or break other people's relationships, and she uses it.

Violet tries to distract herself, grabbing her bookbag off the floor and sliding away from Tonya on the bed. She leans her back against the wall and starts sorting through her things. "He's okay. I remember in middle school he was such a geek. I don't know if he's that good looking now, but his personality makes him attractive. Do you like him?" *Or do you just wanna screw it up for Teah?*

"I could. I don't know. I just think he can do better than Teah Miller. Does Desmond have soccer practice today?" Tonya moves her laptop onto the bed and flips so that she's lying on her stomach, her back to Violet.

Good. Change of subject. "Yup. Monday through Friday. Well, practice some days and games other days, but soccer every day."

"Where's he going to college?"

"He doesn't know yet. His mom wants him to stay in-state, but I think he kind of wants to go to Brown. That's where his dad went."

"Well, you and Desmond better stay friends when he goes to college. I want in on those college parties!"

This is the first jab. *What the hell?!!* "Ummm, I'm kind of hoping we'll still be going out next year." Violet feels blindsided. *This girl is crazy.*

Tonya logs out of her Facebook and begins to shut down her laptop. "Ooookaaay," she says with a smile. "You don't think that when he goes to college he's gonna want some freedom? I mean, I know he's totally into you, but when you go to college after next year, aren't you gonna kinda want a fresh start?" Tonya shoves the laptop aside and strolls across the room to her desk, where she casually flops into a chair facing Violet.

Fresh start? Violet just stares at Tonya for a minute, then, "seriously? Did you seriously just say that?"

"What?" Tonya asks, looking confused. "I'm not trying to say anything bad about you. But you know how college girls are. They're gonna be all over him. I mean, do you even wanna have to worry about that?" She catches Violet's glare, and clarifies, "it's gonna be the same when you go to college." Then, with a shrug, "you're pretty."

Oh no, you didn't. I'm 'pretty.' And you're just freaking fabulous, right? Violet can picture it. Right now, Desmond just has the same old girls to look at most of the time, but college is gonna be a whole other story. "So, basically you're saying I should just give up now, cause it's a losing battle anyway?" There is ice in her tone.

"Noooo," Tonya rolls her eyes expansively. "I don't know why you're trying to turn this into a fight, Violet. All I said is I wanna go to college parties, and you're acting like I just stole your boyfriend. God, sorry I said anything."

The eye roll almost clenched it, but the reference to stealing Violet's boyfriend is what really puts her over the edge. When they first met Desmond, Violet and Tonya both thought he was hot. It was a miracle that he asked Violet out instead of Tonya. Of course, Tonya acted like it was no big deal. She was like, *oh, I could never have lasted with him anyway. He's too goody goody.* But Violet always knew it irked Tonya that she wasn't the one. And here it is. "No, actually Tonya, you're the only one who said anything about stealing my boyfriend. Is it the college parties you want, or the college Desmond you want?"

"Oh please. I wouldn't want Desmond if he was the last man on earth. I mean, he might be nice to look at, but that's about it. I'd take a guy with personality over that plastic man any day." She says it with a smirk, and Violet wants to smack her face.

So now you're dissing me **and** *my man? Bitch.* "Whatever." Violet starts to pack up her things at this point, not even looking at Tonya. "All I'm gonna say is, you better keep your freaking claws off my man, Medusa."

"Pfft. Whatever. You know, you probably don't have to worry about college. You two are so obsessed with each other, I'm sure no one's even gonna wanna bother with him. God, you really need to get a life." She still sits in her chair, just watching Violet, unperturbed.

"Whatever. Bye." Violet marches out of the room and out to the front porch, mind spinning.

Violet stands on the front porch, back rigid and hands clenched, waiting for her ride. Several cars go by, probably people coming home from work. A woman in a track suit jogs past. Across the street, a couple with a stroller and a dog walk past, smiling as they go. Violet's irritated with her friend, but she also knows that Tonya has been hurt by guys before. She can't help but think that Tonya tries to make light of Violet's relationships so that she won't get hurt too. Why else would she be so cruel?

Violet's older sister Maggie pulls up in Mom's Jeep, and Violet slips down the steps and strides through the grass to the car. Maggie's had her license for a few months now, but doesn't have her own car yet. Dad keeps saying he'll get her one, but who knows when, or if, that is going to happen. Maggie is a lot like Violet's mom. She's responsible, organized, sane... She has her future all mapped out. Like Desmond, she's in the process of researching colleges to figure out where she wants to go. She stresses about not getting accepted, but everyone knows she'll get in wherever she wants. She'll go in-state somewhere, because out-of-state would cost too much, and Maggie is not one to throw money away. Not even someone else's money. She always complains when Violet asks Mom or Dad for things, but Violet figures that's what parents are for.

2

Violet looks in the bathroom mirror, and she doesn't like what she sees. She's a pretty girl, tall and curvy, but like a lot of 16-year-olds (like a lot of people, for that matter), it can be hard for her to see herself that way. She has long, straight, dark brown hair, hazel eyes, and a light smattering of freckles over her cheeks and nose. She leans into the mirror, assessing her complexion. "God, I hate my skin."

"Shut up, Vi," mutters Maggie, putting away her comb and hair straightener. Both girls have naturally straight hair, but using the straightener gives it that extra smooth look. "Get ready and quit feeling bad for yourself."

Violet and Maggie share a bathroom with two sinks, but they try hard not to be in there at the same time. Violet spends more time in the mirror criticizing herself than primping, though she doesn't really stress about it. Maggie averages an hour a day on hair and makeup alone. It's fun sometimes when Maggie gets into those moods when she wants to fix her sister up, but that doesn't happen very often. Today is apparently not going to be one of those days.

Maggie strolls out of the bathroom, leaving Violet to contemplate her less than satisfactory reflection a little longer. *Whatever. I shouldn't worry so much about how I look anyway. You're gorgeous, Violet Sanders. And if anybody says different, screw them!* Normally the girls take the bus to school, but sometimes on Tuesdays Mom meets her friends for coffee a couple blocks away, so she drops the girls off instead. Violet begins her morning routine, with 15 minutes until Mom pulls out. Brush teeth, wash face, brush hair. Back to the bedroom to dress. Look in the closet – nothing. Look in the dresser – nothing. Look on the chair. *Damn, I meant to wash those jeans yesterday. Whatever, they look clean.* Look around… desk, bed, bedroom floor, closet floor. *God, why do I have no clothes?* 2 minutes and counting. Violet pulls out the pile of clothes that has gotten itself stuffed between her bed and the wall, and finds a clean shirt that's not too wrinkled. Or at least, it kind of looks like it's supposed to be wrinkled. She throws it on and grabs her sandals, which she can put on in the car.

Today promises to be another boring day. Desmond has soccer practice after school, and half the time after that he's doing homework or researching colleges, so he probably won't be around. Cecilia has dance. As Violet climbs into the car, she considers whether or not she wants to ask Tonya to hang out. Sometimes when they hang out, Violet feels totally invisible. Or, not invisible, but like cardboard. Tonya needs an audience. When Tonya wants to play therapist or best friend, that works out great. She's totally focused and wants to know everything. When Tonya wants to play adventurer, that can be great too. Tons of fun. But when Tonya wants to play poor, pitiful me, or queen of the world, that's not always so great. As far as Violet is concerned, Tonya has gotten into a lot of tough situations, and she needs good friends who can listen to her and support her and give her good advice. It's just tiring sometimes. Like what's going on with Violet doesn't even count, because it can't even *begin* to compare to what's going on in Tonya's life. *Whatever. I have nothing else to do. I'm gonna ask Tonya if she wants to hang.*

Violet sits behind Maggie in their Jeep Cherokee with her head resting on the seat back, watching the world go by. She loves riding in the car. Riding alone with Mom sucks, because Mom always feels the need to discuss something, usually something Violet needs to do, should have done, or better never do again. But when Mom and Maggie are up front together, they pretty much keep each other entertained. All Violet has to do is throw out a "yeah" or "mhmm" every once in awhile.

Violet's relationship with Mom is totally different from Maggie's. She never seems to mess up. Mom treats her more like a friend than a daughter, and Maggie likes it that way. They discuss issues and problems like adults. Violet wants her mother to trust and respect her, but she wants her to be there for her too. Violet doesn't want to have a mature conversation with Mom when she has a problem, she just wants Mom to hug her and tell her it'll be okay. Unfortunately for Violet, that is not Mom's style. As far as Mom is concerned, if you have a problem and you don't know how to fix it, come talk to me. But if you're just feeling bad, snap out of it. Life is tough - deal with it. That's why Violet has always gone to Dad with her problems. He's not exactly a good listener, but at least he'll give you a hug.

The car eases past Littleleaf Elementary School on the edge of their neighborhood, an old, flat, dark brick building with too few windows, but lots of outdoor space. Violet remembers climbing on the big oak tree during recess. That was where she was when she first laid eyes on Cecilia, in the third grade. It was hot out that day, only two weeks after summer break. Violet was laying across a large limb on her stomach, legs wrapped around the tree for support, arms dangling down, moving ever so slightly to help her balance. Her cheek rested against the limb as her eyes tracked the movements of a tiny army of ants far below her. Then squash! Tonya's purpled booted foot crashed down on the procession as she leapt towards the tree.

"Violet, come down!" She called with excitement.

"What?" Violet responded, simultaneously annoyed at the interruption of her study and vaguely aroused by the possibility of new adventure. Even in the third grade, Tonya was already good for an adventure.

"There's a new girl that doesn't speak ANY English! I bet she's never even been in school before. You have *got* to see this." Tonya's eyes twinkled mischievously.

Violet furrowed her brow, trying to imagine what this girl could possibly be doing at a place like Littleleaf. "Really?" She grabbed the tree limb and swung her legs around, plopping onto the ground like playdough. "Where?"

Tonya was fairly jumping for joy. "Right there!" She grabbed Violet's wrist in one hand as she pointed to the far end of the playground with the other. "See her, with Miss Warsaw? Let's wait til she's alone, then go look at her." Tonya was giggling.

The girl wore a frilly white dress and white shoes. Her hair was pulled back in a thick braid. Miss Warsaw was talking to her and pointing at different things in the playground, but the girl just stood with her hands clasped politely in front of her, watching Miss Warsaw, looking rather lost.

"Why should we wait til she's alone?" Violet had challenged. "She looks like she could use a friend. Let's go." Violet marched straight at the girl without a glance back toward Tonya, who practically skipped behind her to check out this strange new addition to the third grade.

Miss Warsaw looked relieved when Violet and Tonya approached, and introduced the new girl as "Cecilia. She just moved here from Venezuela, and I bet she would love it if you girls would show her around." It turned out Tonya was wrong. Cecilia spoke a little English, enough to make introductions, and she had clearly been in school before. It wasn't long before Cecilia was sitting with Violet in the advanced reading groups, smiling encouragingly to Tonya from afar. At first, Tonya was condescending toward Cecilia, which made Violet all the more solicitous of the gentle newcomer. And by the time it registered for Tonya that Cecilia didn't play those games, wasn't phased by Tonya's "funny" comments about her accent or her girly clothes, it was too late for her to back away. The three girls had already become fast friends.

Around one more corner, and Mom turns the jeep out onto the new four lane road. It was only a few years ago that this was just a two lane road with no traffic lights, but that has all changed. Violet looks in passing cars for people she knows. She leans over to scan the crowd on the corner at the entrance to Tonya's neighborhood, where they wait for the bus. *There's Evan.* Even though it's only a few minutes down the street from Violet's neighborhood, it's a different bus route. As she scans the crowd, she thinks about a weird text she got from an unknown number yesterday. It read: ik u hav a bf, but I had 2 tell u how nice and SUPER HOT u r. ur an awesome person. wuz waitn 4 u 2 b single. stil waitn… ur secret admirer :) She figured it was a joke and didn't bother to text back. Still, it's got her curious.

Violet normally rides the bus with Cecilia, who lives a few minutes by car in the opposite direction from Tonya. Cecilia lives in a neighborhood a lot like Violet's: older, smaller homes with big yards. Tonya lives in a big, new subdivision with fancy houses, a pool, clubhouse, tennis courts, but the houses are practically on top of each other. She's an only child and spoiled as hell.

Mom turns right onto Dover, not much to see on this old street, then left onto Thompson Pond Lane, which takes them straight to Thompson Park High School. The high school kind of goes with Tonya's neighborhood. It's 6 years old, two stories, light and bright, all new sports facilities. Violet had been excited about starting high school here, but it turns out high school is high school no matter where you go. And the old high school on the other side of town where she would have gone has a bigger auditorium with a much better arts program. When Violet's eyes hit the school today, she remembers the math assignment she's supposed to turn in first period. *Shit, I hope Cecilia got here early.*

3

Rachel closes her eyes and takes several slow, deep breaths as the line continues to ring, unanswered. She has a million things to do today, and she knows David doesn't work on Mondays. *Come on, David, just answer the phone.* If she has to leave the office to pick Violet up from auditions, she'll have to skip coffee with the ladies tomorrow, and she really wants to get their thoughts on Maggie's college essay. It's a good first draft, but it needs something more and she's not sure what. David's voicemail picks up. *Forget it.* She hits END and sticks her cell phone back in the desk drawer. Her desk is neat, and if you didn't know better you would think she just had to punch a few buttons to be done for the day, but there is always more work to be done. Everything neatly filed, labeled, stamped with a due date. Lots of work to be done. Almost without pause, Rachel rests her fingers on the spreadsheet to her left and lets her other hand dance across the computer keyboard as she pieces together the precise distribution of numbers that will make her client's business thrive, just as her business always has.

■ ■ ■

Violet twists around in her seat to see Cecilia and Tonya smiling at her from the back righthand corner of the auditorium. They've come to offer moral support during today's auditions. Cecilia can only be here today cause she has dance Tuesday and Wednesday. Tonya has said she'll be here all three days, but Violet feels sure she'll think of some reason that she can't come after today. It doesn't matter. She was secretly afraid that Tonya was gonna change her mind and decide to audition herself. She was in the play with Violet last year. She's really not into singing or dancing or acting, but she tried out anyway and made it. It's annoying doing things like this with Tonya, because she never takes it seriously. It's all a big game to her, and that gets on Violet's nerves. This is Violet's whole future, not just something she does to kill time. She returns her friends' smiles and turns back around to watch the next singer audition. Today is voice, tomorrow is dance, and Wednesday is callbacks. Violet is happy, nervous, and excited.

The girl two seats down from her gets up and walks toward the stage. Everyone is going up in the order they are seated, but there are a lot of empty seats. No one wants to sit too close to the competition, so only pretty good friends are sitting side by side. Sarah sits immediately to Violet's right. She's an awesome dancer with a great stage presence, but her voice is only so so. "Almost our turn," whispers Violet.

"I'm nervous."

Violet can hear it in her voice. "You'll do great." She would be more encouraging if she weren't about to audition herself. The piano plays an introduction. Lips move on stage, but no lyrics are forthcoming. *You can do it. Oh shit, you can do it.* Violet knows the girl by sight, but doesn't know her name. She's a freshman this year. Her brow is creased and her cheeks are flushed. Her lips move again, and she croaks out a few words, "had me a bla-ast". *Breathe… nice and easy.* The girls gaze moves up into the empty balcony, and her voice grows stronger. "Met a boy, cute as can beeee." She's found her rhythm. The voice is still a little shaky, but she's singing now. "Summer days, drifting away…" she finishes the stanza, fingers intertwined in a savage dance at her pelvis.

"Thank you. Good job," the director calls out, looking at his notes. "Next!" He looks up to see who is coming.

Violet strides toward the stairs at stage right as the other girl scurries down the stairs at stage left. She inhales deeply to calm her nerves. She is not smiling now.

"Violet?" inquires the director when she reaches center stage.

"Hi," Violet nods. "Violet Sanders."

"What piece have you chosen for today, Violet?" The director is neither warm nor cold. Violet figures it's good that at least he remembers her name. She's taken chorus and dance electives, but she hasn't taken a theater elective yet, so she only knows him from being in the school musicals the past couple of years.

"Beauty School Drop-Out." Violet feels more confident now that she's up on stage. She knows she can sing, she just has to make her face and body talk while she does it. The pianist begins to play, and Violet struts forward. Her voice is soft yet powerful as she begins. This is where she belongs. This is what she does. Her eyes roam the dark theater, pulling the audience in. "No graduation, day for you..." She's only allowed to sing the first two verses, so she kicks it into high gear. "...to have the doctor fix your nose up!" *Ooops.* She hit all the notes, but that last pose she tried to strike wasn't exactly spot on. Violet feels awkward and conspicuous as she resumes a neutral posture.

"Ok. Thanks." Again, neither warm nor cold. Just another singer among many.

Damn, I really wanted a good role this year. Violet feels her eyes grow moist as she flashes a rapid half-smile at the director. She drops her head and scurries off stage left, no better than the freshman who could barely get the words out. She lifts her head when she hits the aisle and heads straight for the exit, knowing Tonya and Cecilia will be right behind her.

"You did it!" Cecilia squeals. "That was awesome!" The girls exit the auditorium all at once, like an amoeba.

"That was amaaaaazing." Tonya grabs her shoulders from behind and gives her a friendly shake. The positive energy begins to rub off on Violet and she smiles.

"Uggh, I hate auditions," she moans playfully. Violet can tell her friends are not just being nice. They really were impressed. "I'm ready to get out of here, though. You guys still coming back to my house?" The girls walk toward the lockers.

"Yup," agrees Tonya.

"Of course." Cecilia puts her arm around Violet's shoulders as they walk. "You better get a lead this year. No one sings better than you do."

"I am pretty amazing, aren't I?" Violet jokes. *Who cares if I don't get a lead. I can still get a hot solo.*

"Wow, confident much?" Tonya laughs with her.

"You *are* amazing, actually." Cecilia knows how to laugh and have fun, but she also knows how to read people and cares enough to pay attention. She's a straight shooter. She tells it like it is when it needs to be said, but she does it so sweetly that you don't get offended. And if you need a confidence boost, she can do that too.

Violet smiles at Cecilia. "I love you, girl."

"So how are we getting back to your house?" Tonya asks, the audition already forgotten.

"My mom said to call her and she'll come get us, but she might not be able to come right away." As Violet turns the knob on her combination lock, she realizes that she doesn't actually need anything out of her locker. She opens it up anyway and a folded piece of printer paper sails to the floor. She snatches it up and holds it inside her locker to read it:

> Good luck at auditions. I know you'll rock!
> Your Secret Admirer, S.A. :)

Violet crumples the note nonchalantly and stuffs it in her bookbag. *Who is this person?* She pushes things around in the locker for a minute to play it off, then shuts it purposefully, as if she's just accomplished something. *Is it **these** guys, just playing around?* She looks at her friends, and it's obvious they know nothing about a note. *Well, I guess I have a fan, don't I?* She smiles. Apparently the other girls had no need to go to their lockers either, because they all automatically turn and head toward the front door.

"Maybe Marcus can come pick us up and we can stop at the coffee shop on the way back to your house." Tonya is old enough to get her driver's license, but hasn't bothered to even get her permit yet. Cecilia and Violet got their permits almost as soon as they turned 16. "He just got his Dad's old car," continues Tonya.

"My mom usually likes me to ask ahead of time if I'm going to be riding with another teenager, but maybe she won't care today since that means she wouldn't have to leave work early."

"Lemme call him." Tonya has already pulled out her phone and is dialing the number. Violet and Cecilia exchange a look. *Oooookaaaay.* "Marcus, watcha doin?... Come pick me up. I'm with Vi and Cici." Only Tonya calls Cecilia 'Cici.' "At the school. Vi had auditions... Kay! See you in a minute!"

The girls push open the heavy doors and Violet calls her mom. She gets her voicemail. "Hey mom. I'm at school with Cecilia and Tonya. Auditions are over for today. I was wondering if we could ride to the coffee shop with Marcus, and he'll take us home from there. Call me back. Thanks." They plop themselves and their various bags and purses at the bottom of the concrete steps to wait.

"Watcha got goin on in dance these days?" Violet asks Cecilia.

"We have a competition at the end of November. I'm gonna be in two jazz numbers and a hip hop piece, so I've been getting ready for that. We have the craziest costumes for one of them! It's got this long, feathered skirt and a little Chiquita Banana top. It's crazy. I wanna wear my hair curly with a high pony tail for that one, but I don't know if I'll have time to put it up for the other numbers afterward." Cecilia is naturally bronze skinned, and still has some of her summer tan. She has thick, dark hair with layer after layer of luscious spiral curls, but she usually wears it straight. She's proud to be Latina, but she wouldn't mind some of Violet's naturally straight "white girl" hair sometimes.

Violet looks through the glass front doors of the school and notices Sarah, Julie, and Moses heading toward the exit. Her mind goes back to auditions, and her phone buzzes in her pocket. She pulls it out and looks at it to see that it's a text from mom, but she turns her attention to the doors again and catches Sarah's eye as she walks out. "How'd it go?" she calls.

"Pretty good, I think. You sounded great."

"Thanks. I'm sure you did great. Sorry I didn't stay. I just got nervous after I sang, for some reason, and I had to get outta there."

"I know what you mean. I got outta there as soon as I was done too." Sarah's friends are down the steps and getting into a car that just pulled up. "See ya tomorrow!"

"Bye!" Violet waves, then looks down to read her text message:

be home by 6 if you have homework, and don't forget you need to vacuum.

Tryouts were great, mom. Thanks for asking. She puts her phone away as another car pulls up, "Mom's cool with us going to the coffee shop. Here's Marcus. Let's go."

Violet and Cecilia head toward the backseat. They're friendly with Marcus, but they don't know him as well as Tonya does. He's a senior at Thompson Park and has had some classes with Maggie. Tonya jumps into the front passenger seat. "Hey! Let's go to the coffee shop," she says to Marcus, as if the idea just occurred to her.

"Cool," he replies. He would probably do whatever Tonya asked without thinking twice; that's just how it is with her and guys. Violet loves how Tonya can make plans that require other people's cooperation without even stopping to think that they might object. Okay, so she doesn't love it. Actually, it drives her crazy, but it's convenient at times like these. Marcus pulls the car out. "Everybody doin aright?"

"Awesome," Tonya seems to answer for all of them.

"Hey, Violet, how's Desmond?" Marcus asks. "He still playing soccer?"

"Yeah. How bout you?" Desmond goes to private school, but he's always known a lot of public school kids from his various sports. Violet doesn't really care if Marcus plays soccer. *I wonder if Desmond can meet us at the coffee shop?*

"Naah, I quit like two years ago, girl. I'll be playing basketball, though." Marcus has a habit of looking at you through the rearview mirror while he drives. It's rather unnerving. Violet was looking forward to hanging out with Tonya and Cecilia, and she finds she's not appreciating this friendly intrusion. Luckily, Tonya is more than happy to take over the small talk.

While Tonya entertains Marcus in the front seat, Violet turns to hear Cecilia better. "Huh?"

Cecilia repeats her question at the same low volume now that Violet's not distracted. "You goin to your dad's this weekend?"

"Yeah, we're goin Sunday." She's supposed to see her Dad this weekend, but there's no telling if he'll come through. Hopefully, the visit will happen, and hopefully he won't be too drunk to notice the girls are there. Dad has tried sobriety before, but it never seems to last very long. Violet tells herself she doesn't really care, but deep down she knows she does. Violet's friends know a little bit about her dad. Cecilia and Tonya were both around in the fourth grade when Violet's parents divorced, and she used to tell them about Dad going to AA and stuff in the fifth and sixth grade, back when she thought he might actually stop drinking. Since then, though, she doesn't really talk about him. Why would she? Her friends actually like him, and that's a nice change from Maggie and her mom. A couple of times he's stopped by unannounced when she was hanging with her friends and ordered them pizza or taken them out for ice cream at the drive-in. He never comes by when he's been drinking a lot, and he's funny and laid back, so they have a good time. Desmond is the only one that Violet really talks to about her Dad. He listens, he doesn't judge, and he doesn't think Violet's wrong for loving such a screw up.

4

Rachel ruffles through her drawer looking for a pair of stockings without runs. *Why do I save stockings with runs?* she asks herself as she pulls out a good pair and shuts her drawer. She can hear the girls arguing in the bathroom again. *God, I feel bad for Maggie.* Rachel sits on the edge of her bed to pull on her stockings. She's decided to wear a suit with a skirt to work today. She's meeting a fellow grad student for lunch to discuss a project they're working on together for class. At 38-years-old, Matt is seven years younger than she is, and at least 10-years-younger than the guys she occasionally dates. He's also married with two young children. She likes working with him because she trusts that he is devoted to his family, but he also has a naturally flirtacious personality, and it feels good to be on the receiving end of that. She figures wearing a suit sends the message that she's not interested in any funny business, but the skirt softens it up a little, saying I'm an older professional woman, but I'm still worth looking at. And she is.

Rachel has always been a hard worker. She graduated high school with honors, and went straight to work in the office of a big department store to help support the family. Growing up, Mom ruled the house with an iron fist, stretching Dad's auto mechanic income as far as it would go. They could have been quite comfortable, had Dad not taken money out of his checks for booze and girlfriends before handing the rest over to Mom, his "one and only." *Bullshit.* So Rachel went to work straight out of high school to try and create a better life for her younger brothers than the one she had had. She met David shortly thereafter, and they dated for several years before she agreed to marry him. She got her Bachelor's degree in accounting while making babies with David, started her own business when Maggie was 7, and left David when Violet was 8 and Maggie was 9. She never looked back.

Rachel is a beautiful woman when she laughs, which isn't very often. She'll chuckle or turn up the corners of her mouth, but a real belly laugh is hard to come by. Her body, however, is amazing. While her face can be a little hard, she has beautiful skin, untainted by the elements. She works out religiously, and has long, lean muscles in her arms and legs. Needless to say, she looks good in a skirt. Rachel heads to the bathroom to fix her hair. When she was younger she didn't wear any makeup. Now she always puts a little on her eyes and cheeks, just enough to look professional. She wears her hair in a short bob and gets it cut every eight weeks, like clockwork, same style. Cover the grey, trim off the ends. She blows her hair dry at night to straighten it, and just needs to run a comb through it in the morning. As she looks at herself in the mirror today, she wonders if she can do something to spice it up. Uninspired, she follows her usual routine.

Rachel finds herself smiling as she gathers her things to head out the door. It's nice to have something besides work going on. *Matt. Why can't my suitors be as interesting as him?* She pictures him smiling as he talks about his children, and then she thinks of David. David, who couldn't even remember Violet's name the first three days she was alive. David, who criticizes Maggie for not going to enough parties. "You're only young once. You need to enjoy it!" *Yeah, David, well you're not young anymore, so what's your excuse?* Rachel is no longer smiling. She thinks about her girls going to David's house this Sunday. She thinks about all that Maggie does trying to change him and take care of him, and she thinks about how much Violet adores him. It hurts and frustrates her that Violet has so much love for her dad, who has done nothing for her, and can't seem to stand the sight of Rachel's face. *You're a jerk, David,* she thinks as she heads downstairs. *You hurt me, that's fine. But grow up and be a man for your daughters.* Rachel grabs her keys and heads out to work.

5

Violet is celebrating. Not Rizzo, but still a Pink Lady! Marty Marschino isn't a lead role, but it's a hundred times better than being in the chorus. She's at Desmond's house with Cecilia, Tonya, Marcus (Tonya's pick of the week), Cecilia's boyfriend Cam, and Desmond's friend Jaden. Desmond lives in a huge house out in the country. Well, it looks like it's out in the country, with a sprawling lawn and wooded backyard with a pond. He only lives 15 minutes away from Violet, though. He's got a big bedroom with a private bathroom, but they are hanging out in the game room tonight. Tonya and Marcus are over by the pool table eyeing the bar. *I hope she knows Desmond will kick her out if she starts to get stupid.* Desmond doesn't mind people coming over to have a few drinks, but he's not letting anyone raid his parents' liquor cabinet, and he's not letting anyone get shitfaced while his parents are around either.

Violet sits with her back against the arm of the leather L-shaped couch, a beer resting in her lap. Her legs are draped over Desmond's legs, and her toes are tucked in between the two seat cushions. Desmond sits upright with one hand resting on Violet's thigh, and his other arm resting on the back of the couch. In that arm, he holds a beer, out of which he takes a final swig and leans over Violet to put his empty on the coffee table. "So Celia, I thought you had dance tonight?"

"I did, but we ended early cause they had to work on one of the pieces that I'm not in. Competition's in two weeks!" Cecilia sits on the other side of the L, leaning against Cam, who's got one arm around her. They've been dating longer than she and Desmond have, and Violet loves how comfortable they seem around each other.

Jaden sits in the corner of the L. Violet can't remember if he's single or not, but he's been paying Cecilia a lot of attention tonight. Cam doesn't seem to notice. "My sister dances," Jaden comments. "Where's your competition?"

Tonya interrupts, walking over with three glasses and a bottle. "I brought wine, ladies. Don't make me drink alone." She turns to Violet, "Vi, drink up!" Violet has been nursing the same beer for at least 45 minutes, and Cecilia hasn't had anything to drink. Tonya opens the clear bottle with a twist top and something light pink inside. She fills the glasses to the top.

"I'll drink to Violet's success!" cheers Cecilia. She sits up to reach for a glass.

"Fine," says Violet, setting her beer on the table and adjusting so she faces her friends. "That beer was nasty anyway." She takes the glass that Tonya extends to her.

Desmond wraps his arms around her and kisses her on the cheek. "You deserve it, beautiful. I'm proud of you."

Damn, I love this boy. She smiles and leans her forehead against his cheek.

"Wait, we wanna drink to you too!" Cam calls, rising from the couch. "What does everybody want?"

"I'm good." Jaden holds up his beer to show Cam.

"I'll take another beer, man. Thanks." Desmond holds Violet close, and she's glad of it. She likes how relaxed Cecilia and Cam are with each other, but she doesn't exactly understand it. When Violet is around Desmond, she wants to be close to him every second. To feel his arms around her, to run her hands over his muscular chest and arms and shoulders. She likes to play her finger tips over his rough hair, shaved almost to the scalp. Being in his arms makes her feel safe and warm and special, like all is right with the world. And when she's not around him, she wishes she were.

Two bottlecaps pop over by the bar. Cam hands one to Desmond, then stands next to Violet and holds his beer arm up. "To Violet, best actress in Morris County."

"To Violet!" they echo. Violet smiles, one of the big grins that her mom has such a hard time achieving. *I have good friends.* She sips her drink. *Sweet. Tastes like Kool Aid.* She sips again.

■ ■ ■

Desmond has been at the pool table for awhile. Nobody can really compete with him, since he has a pool table in his house and has been playing forever. Violet likes to watch the way the light plays off the dark skin on his slender arms when he sets up a shot. Then again, he's set up a whole lot of shots tonight.

Tonya sits down next to Violet and leans into her. "Me and Marcus are gonna go out for a smoke after this game. You wanna come?"

Violet feels her stomach muscles clench for a fraction of a second, and worry flashes across her face. "Does Desmond know?"

"I didn't say anything. We'll go way back in the woods where nobody can see us."

"He's gonna smell it when you come back. Hang on and lemme talk to him."

"Kay. You think Jaden smokes?"

"I doubt it, but I really don't know. I mean, I guess if we're gonna go we should offer it to everybody, even though we know at least two of them are gonna say no."

"Yeah, we should. There goes your man again."

Violet looks to see that Desmond and Marcus have finished up their game. Cam is standing by to play winner. "Desmond, can I talk to you for a minute?"

"Yeah." Desmond starts to walk toward the couch, but Violet takes his arm and leads him down the stairs. "What's up?"

Violet's hands are sweating. She knows Desmond is against drugs, and it's really not that big a deal, but she wouldn't mind a smoke. "So I guess

Marcus brought some weed, and we were wondering if we could go down by the pond for a smoke…" She holds her body tense as she waits to see if she's going to regret the question.

Desmond leans against the wall and looks at her. "You wanna smoke?" His face is impassive.

He is so serious. "Just a couple of hits. I wouldn't mind some fresh air anyway." Violet realizes she's making excuses. *Yes, I wanna smoke! Is it really that big a deal?*

Desmond stands up, takes her face in his hands, and kisses her gently. "Go smoke," he says softly. "But don't stay away from me too long."

Awww. "You're tremendous," she smiles at him. "I won't,"

Violet, Tonya, Marcus, Jaden, and Cam head outside. It turns out Jaden does smoke, and Cam apparently wants some fresh air. He used to smoke every once in awhile during summer, but Violet hasn't seen him do it since school started back. It's cool out tonight, and Violet wishes she had on something warmer than this sweatshirt.

"You got it ready, or you need to roll it?" asks Jaden.

"It's clean, but…" Marcus pulls a cigar out of his jacket. "Anybody wanna do the honors?"

Violet walks with her head down, knowing the question is not for her.

"Nah, that's all you man," encourages Jaden.

"Damn, I gotta bring the weed *and* roll the blunt," Marcus jokes. "Shit, you guys are making me work!"

Violet watches Marcus split open the cigar and toss the guts on the ground in the woods. She keeps walking for a minute before it dawns on her how obvious that pile of tobacco is. She turns back and uses her feet to mix the tobacco into the leaves, then jogs to catch back up with the others. Cam turns to look at her and winks. He gets it. The others didn't even notice she had stopped.

"I need a place to sit down." Marcus again.

"There's a couple of places to sit by the pond," Violet suggests. The group walks on purposefully. She wonders if this is where she should be, out in the cold dark night while her boyfriend and best friend are left alone. Not that she's worried about them doing anything, just maybe it's not too cool that she left them.

The trees open up onto a large, deep pond. It's a dark night, with hardly any moon. Marcus and Tonya sit down on a rock together while Violet, Cam, and Jaden look out at the water.

"This is amazing, isn't it?" Cam asks.

"Yeah, we come out here and swim sometimes in the summer." Jaden points off toward the right bank. "There used to be a branch hanging over the pond over there, with a rope tied onto it. When we were little we used to swing out and jump into the pond." He laughs as he remembers. "I guess we didn't know when to stop, though, cause we broke that thing in half like two years ago. The branch, I mean. I guess it wasn't as big as it seemed when we were younger."

The strong smell of marijuana hits Violet, and she and her friends turn around simultaneously. Marcus is looking at them as he pulls on the blunt, eyes squinted against the smoke. He stands up and walks over with the blunt extended to Jaden. Jaden smokes, then passes it to Violet. It's strong stuff, and Violet's not used to smoking blunts. She realizes before she's even inhaled that she took too big of a pull. She tries to finish inhaling through her cough. *Awkward.* She passes the blunt to Tonya.

Tonya's laughing when she takes the blunt. She says to no one in particular, "we need to keep an eye on Violet. She's not used to smoking good weed."

Marcus offers the blunt to Cam a couple of times, but he politely declines. He walks up the bank a little, and Violet is struck with how easy it is for him to say no. How many times has Violet said, I'm only gonna have one beer tonight, or I'm not gonna smoke this week, and she does it anyway? *This is good weed, though. Kinda scary actually.* Violet is used to feeling silly when she smokes, kind of ditsy, but tonight she feels foggy and excited all at the same time. Like she wants to run around the pond, climb a tree, and jump into the lake, but her brain's moving too slow to actually get her anywhere. She feels herself swaying involuntarily, and wonders if the others can see it or if it's mostly in her head.

"You like that?" asks Marcus, his eyes fixed on her.

Violet looks at him unsteadily. She doesn't know Marcus that well. "That's good stuff," she replies, trying to sound like her normal self. She can't tell if she's pulling it off or not. "You guys about ready to go back?" She looks around at everybody. She can feel Marcus's eyes still fixed on her.

Tonya walks over and loops her arm into Violet's. "You guys go on," she says to Cam and Jaden. "I want to talk to my girl for a sec."

Cam and Jaden look at each other, and Marcus swiftly takes over. "Let's head back toward the house, and I'll walk back in a minute to get the girls." It would sound fishy, but Jaden's pretty well loaded, and Cam's been ready to go back for awhile.

Tonya drags Violet over to sit on the rock as the boys walk away. "What did you think?" she smiles at Violet, eyes glassy.

"It was good. Why?"

"You liked it?!!"

This girl is acting like she just discovered America. "Yeah…" Violet is trying to give Tonya a hard stare, but it's not really working. *This weed is crazy.* "Why?"

"You'll see in a minute." Tonya turns to look toward the house.

The longer she sits, the more messed up Violet feels, like the weed molecules are mysteriously multiplying in her brain. Before she knows it, Marcus is already coming back out of the woods.

"I ditched them about halfway to the house," he announces. "Did you tell her?"

"I figured I'd let you."

Violet is curious, a little nervous, and a little excited. *What is going on?*

"So you're getting ready to be a big actress, huh?" Marcus squeezes in next to Violet on the rock.

"Not really." *Okay, what the fuck is going on?*

"You feeling pretty good?" Marcus is taking his sweet time with this. Violet can feel Tonya's restlessness on the other side of her.

Tonya grabs Violet's arm and squeezes firmly, smiling coyly at her. "You ever try coke before?"

Violet jumps up gracelessly from the rock and tumbles forward onto her knees. "No!" *Oh my God, does she have coke?!! What the hell? She knows I'm not into that shit!* Violet turns onto her bottom before trying to stand up again. "Did you guys bring coke?!!" *Desmond is going to flip!* Violet's thoughts are all scrambled. Tonya looks hurt, all of sudden, and Marcus just looks amused.

"Congratu-frickin-lations to you too," Tonya pouts. "I thought it would be a nice surprise. You don't have to act all shocked by it." Violet is pissed, but she doesn't know what to say.

Marcus puts his arm around Tonya. "It's alright, girl. She didn't mean it like that. She was just surprised."

Why the hell is he making excuses for me? Yes, I did mean it like that! She makes it to her feet with some difficulty. *Damn, I'm high.*

"Violet, why don't you try just enjoying yourself instead of always trying to show off for your goody two shoes boyfriend? I mean, with Cecilia I get it. She's not into partying, but you used to do a lot of stuff before Desmond came into the picture. You know why that weed was so good?"

Even in her confusion, Violet is beginning to put two and two together. *Fuck, please don't say what I think you're gonna say.*

Tonya's face has turned cold. She's not pouting anymore. "Yes, actually you *have* done coke before. And I'm pretty sure you liked it." She turns to Marcus. "Can we do some lines now?"

Violet is frozen. Thoughts start to form in her head, but she cannot put them together. Her lips move to speak, but there is nothing to say. She turns unsteadily and looks at the cold pond, and she thinks about walking into it. That would make sense. She would be wet and cold... simple. What she is feeling right now is not so simple. *I hate Tonya. I hate this. I wish I was sober. I can't stand this. I'm an idiot. Why did I do that? I hate myself.* She turns to look back at Tonya and Marcus.

Tonya is otherwise occupied, but Marcus looks back at her. "It's just coke, girl. It's really not a big deal." Violet wills her feet to take her back to the house.

6

When Violet gets back to the house, Desmond is sitting stone faced on the living room couch, in the dark, waiting for her. "Hey," she ventures.

"Where are Tonya and Marcus?" he asks without looking at her.

Violet is nervous and disoriented. *Why is Desmond mad at me?* She had thought she could come back and curl up in his lap and he would make these yucky feelings go away. Instead, she feels like she is being attacked again. "They're coming." She had wanted to tell him about the cocaine, but this doesn't seem like such a good time. "Where is everybody?"

"Jaden's in the game room watching t.v.; Cam and Cecilia left as soon as he got back." He turns to look at her now. "You know you've been gone over an hour and a half?"

Violet is still standing in the doorway. *Shit.* "No, I didn't know it was that long." Violet feels her stomach sink. She needs to sit down, but Desmond clearly doesn't want her near him. He is staring straight ahead again. She slides over to the near wall and sits down on the floor, pulling her knees up to her chin. "I'm sorry." *So much for my celebration.*

"How are you getting home tonight?"

Violet also stares straight ahead, dazed and unfocused. *I thought you were taking me.* "I don't know. I'll see if Marcus can give me a ride."

"Fine." They are both silent for a moment. The darkness fills the space between them like a black hole, sucking away all sense of connection, of belonging. Desmond stands up. "I'm going to bed. Lemme know if Marcus can't drive you." He walks toward the stairs and leaves her.

Violet continues to stare blankly ahead, sensing his departure more than seeing it. *What the hell?* She can't quite wrap her head around how her simple celebration has suddenly turned into an emotional battlefield. She cries silently, warm drops sliding down her cheek, wet snot trying to drip from her left nostril. She pulls her sweatshirt over her hand and uses it to wipe her nose. She doesn't bother to dry the tears that continue to fall freely. She is like an ice cube melting in the clenched fist of a runner who has just lost the race.

■ ■ ■

Desmond walks upstairs stoically, hoping that Violet will follow. He thought he would be driving her home, and is disappointed that after spending all evening in the woods without him, now she doesn't even want him to take her home. He knows he has been focused on his college search, and wonders if she is getting tired of him. She seems so into him when they're together, but she can turn on him so easily. She didn't even come to him when she got back inside. He never knows what he's going to get with her. He can't be like Marcus. He doesn't want to be like Marcus. But is that what Violet wants?

He slumps into his bedroom and dumps himself on the bed. He can still see Violet sitting on the living room floor, stoned out of her mind. Violet is so easily impressed. What does she see in Tonya? If that's really the lifestyle she wants, getting drunk and high and having a different boyfriend every time you turn around, she can have it. That's not what Desmond is looking for. Desmond wants the girl he saw in the coffee shop on Monday. The girl who can't wait to tell him about her audition. Who is impressed that he remembers which pastry she likes, and asks *him* to fix her coffee because no one else gets the cream and sugar just right. He wants the girl who lies next to him in bed in her t-shirt and panties without a care in the world, because she knows that she is everything to him and he would never hurt or disrespect her.

Desmond hears a door open downstairs, and wonders if it's Tonya and Marcus coming in, or Violet going out to find them. He eases over to the door and cracks it open to listen. He hears voices on the stairs, laughing. It's Tonya and Marcus, then Violet's voice, quiet and clear, "Guys, we gotta go. Desmond went to bed."

Tonya is not so quiet. "What?!! The party's just starting! Where is he?" Footsteps coming down the hall.

"T, stop. He's not in the mood." Closer now. He wants to go to her. But what does she want? He thinks she sounds sad. Should he go to her?

"Oh my God. He is such a nerd!" The footsteps move away.

"Come on, Tonya. We'll find something to do." Marcus now. "Violet, you in?"

He listens to the footsteps fade. He can't hear Violet's answer, so he follows. Down the stairs and out into the hallway. The front door is about to close, and without thinking Desmond calls out, "Hey!" Marcus pokes his head in. "Where's Violet?"

Marcus walks outside calling her name, and a moment later she is standing in the doorway. Her face is drawn, but in the dim light Desmond can't see that she's been crying. "You want me to drive you home?"

"Whatever." Flat. Cold. She needed Desmond, and he turned his back on her. She didn't mean to be gone so long. She didn't know. "I'm sure Marcus will take me." *I hope. God I don't wanna be stuck hangin out with them all night.*

Desmond is silent for a moment, and then, "what if I want to take you?" He needs her to need him. He can't stand to feel so useless, like he's not good enough for her.

She shrugs, "then take me." She looks at him, challenging, yet silently hoping he'll take a stand for her. *Please take me home, Desmond.*

"Well, do you wanna go home or do you wanna hang out with them?" He won't show her his cards. She has to decide what she wants.

"I wanna go home."

It's not the answer he sought, but it's close enough. "Hang on." Desmond turns and heads back toward the living room to get his keys.

Violet walks outside, shutting the door behind her. Tonya and Marcus are already at his car. They are both wired. Violet has never seen anyone on cocaine before, and she doesn't like it. Tonya seems jumpy, and even less inhibited than usual. When did she start using cocaine, and what else is she using? "You guys can go. Desmond's gonna to take me home." *Thank God.*

"Bye!" yells Tonya, as she turns around and gets into the car. She's not disappointed to be rid of Violet for the evening.

"Congratulations on the play," Marcus adds. "Tell Desmond thanks, it was real." And they're off.

Violet leans against the porch column just as Desmond walks out. "They said thanks."

He walks up behind her and puts his arms around her. "You sure you didn't wanna go with them?"

"No. They rolled a blunt and put cocaine in it without telling any-body." *Shit, I don't know if I shoulda said that. He already doesn't like Tonya.*

"What?" Violet feels Desmond's body go tense. He turns her around and looks her in the eye. "What did you say?"

She turns her head away from his intense gaze and repeats, "they rolled a blunt with cocaine in it and didn't tell us." *God, I'm an idiot.* "Then when Cam and Jaden went back to the house, they tried to get me to snort coke with them."

He shakes his head, looking toward the road where they just pulled out of sight. "Those are some nice fuckin friends you got, Violet." His voice is hard and cold as stone. "Real nice."

Violet can't read his bitter tone. *Is he mad at me? What the fuck?* She goes cold again. "Yeah, well, I guess they thought I'd like it." She jerks out if his arms and heads down the steps toward the driveway and Desmond's Ford Explorer, given to him new for his 17th birthday last year. "Can we go now?"

Desmond watches her walk away. Like her, he misinterprets the angry response. *Does she actually think it's cool that they did that? Holy shit, she does, doesn't she?* He follows her down the walk and steps around her to open her door, staring hard at the tree line so as not to see her face telling him he's wrong. Not cool enough. Not down. Old-fashioned. A nerd. He shuts her door hard and gets into the driver's seat.

It is a quiet drive home. Violet's high has begun to wear off, and she needs Desmond to be okay with her. When they turn into her neighborhood, she looks into her lap and nearly whispers, "I'm sorry we were gone so long."

Desmond looks back at her, and eases the car over to the curb, putting it in park. "I don't care how long they were gone. They could have been gone all night for all I care. I care about you, Violet. You left me, and you didn't even notice."

Tears again. *I'm such a freaking cry baby.* "I'm sorry."

He reaches over with both hands and pulls her into his chest, wrapping his arms around her and burying his chin in her hair. "It's okay, boo. It's okay. I love you so much."

7

Violet stands uncomfortably in front of the bathroom mirror while Maggie works on straightening her hair. The visit with Dad last weekend didn't happen after all. He had some emergency with his girlfriend's son, supposedly. *Whatever.* So the girls are supposed to go see him this afternoon. Dad has been living with his girlfriend, Donna, in her townhouse for the past six or seven years. When he first moved in with her, her son was living with them part-time, but he moved in with his dad when he turned 16. Donna's pretty cool, and so's her son. She owns a housekeeping business. When the economy was better, she mostly worked from home, but now she does a lot of the cleaning herself.

Violet shifts so that she is leaning against the counter, trying to make her back a little more comfortable. Maggie pulls her hands away and sighs. "Do you want me to do this or not?"

"Sorry." Violet stands upright again, and Maggie resumes her work.

"So you have anything planned for this week?" Maggie asks. Today is Sunday.

"Just rehearsal." *Man this takes forever. How do you do this everyday?* "What about you?"

"Not much. Turn a little bit this way." Maggie likes to hear about what Violet's got going on, but she doesn't usually fill Violet in on her own life.

"You going to visit colleges next weekend?"

"Yeah," Maggie answers. She is focused on Violet's hair, and works methodically from one side of her head to the other. When Violet tries to straighten her own hair, she tends to take a random approach, grabbing sections haphazardly in the hopes that it will all come out straight in the end. Maggie does a much better job.

Violet is getting increasingly restless. "I wonder if Donna will be there today?"

"She's supposed to be. I think they might take us to an AA meeting."

"Great," Violet replies sarcastically. If Dad is going to an Alcoholic's Anonymous meeting tonight, he must have partied hard last weekend. Donna likes to drink, but as far as Violet knows she doesn't have a drinking problem. As far as she can tell, Donna just goes to meetings to socialize. Violet's never been sure exactly why he makes the girls go sometimes, but it's fine. Not exactly a thrilling Sunday evening, but there are some cool people there. 'Old-timers' who used to be as messed up as Dad, some of them a lot worse by the sound of it, and now they've been sober for years. She likes to talk to those guys. She likes to hear their stories. One time Dad accidentally brought the girls to a closed meeting, where only the alcoholic is allowed to attend, so a couple of the old-timers hung out with the girls in the lobby the whole time. That was probably the best time she's ever had hanging out with adults when they weren't actually doing something fun – just hanging.

"Violet, I know you think Dad's drinking is not that big a deal, but it's really messed his life up." *Well, duh.* "If he's trying to do the right thing, we need to support him."

Violet loves her father, but she's done waiting for him to change. If he sobers up for good, that's great. That would be fabulous. But one of the things Violet has learned from listening to those old-timers is that a person stops using when they're ready to stop using, and not a second before. If Dad's gonna stop drinking, it'll be because Dad wants to stop drinking, and not because of anything Violet did or didn't do. Rather than try to convince Maggie of this, she simply responds, "yeah. Hair almost done?"

8

Dinner at Dad's is delicious. Dad has made his famous fall-off-the-bone ribs, with cheesy mashed potatoes and Donna's green bean casserole. Violet sits with her elbows on the table, fingers dripping greasy sauce. She sees Maggie eyeing her skeptically, and she responds by dipping one of those greasy fingers into her mashed potatoes for a taste.

"Good?" Her Dad smiles at her.

"Delicious," Violet smiles in return. The kitchen is warm and cozy. There's no separate dining room in the townhouse, just a dining area with a large table between the open kitchen and the living room. There have been some bad days in this house, but today is a good one. Today, Violet appreciates the slightly out-of-date, flowered wallpaper, the random piles of paper and such scattered here and there, the general aura of contained disarray. Not dirty, just comfortably messy. *Why can't Mom live like this?*

"Maggie, how's the college search going?" Donna is good at small talk. Dad, not so much.

Maggie wipes her hands before reaching for a rib, making Violet chuckle to herself. Maggie scowls at her before responding to Donna, "it's good. I've got a couple of tours lined up, and I'll probably start filling out applications at the end of the month."

"That's great. And you already know what you'll major in?"

Of course she does. She knows what she's going to major in, where she's going to work when she graduates, when she's going to get married, how many kids she's gonna have… She probably already has her burial plot lined up. Violet chuckles to herself again, this time without drawing any attention.

"I'm going to double major in biology and Spanish. I've already taken some Advanced Placement classes, so I think I'll be able to handle it."

"Wow, that's fabulous!" Donna's praise is heartfelt. It doesn't seem to bother her in the least that she never finished college herself, and her 20-year-old son is just now trying to get into a community college. She is sincerely happy for Maggie. Violet admires that about Donna. *I need to be more like that.*

Dad pipes in with, "that's my Maggie. Gonna be a brain surgeon, I bet." The three women all smile politely. Dad should know by now that Maggie plans to be a pediatrician. Has planned it since she was in the 7th grade.

"So are we going to a meeting tonight?" Violet asks as she reaches for her glass of iced tea, covered in smudgy barbecue fingerprints.

"I thought maybe you girls would like to have movie night instead," Dad suggests.

Damn. Violet didn't want to go to a meeting, but she wanted her Dad to want to go. She tells herself that he's fine. He can take care of himself. But in her heart, she is always disappointed when there's some reason to think he might be getting better, and then something happens to tell her he's not. He always goes to meetings when he's trying not to drink.

"Dad." Maggie is using her mommy voice. "Don't you think it would be a good idea to go to a meeting? I thought you were looking for a new sponsor." A sponsor is somebody who has been sober for awhile, who teaches a recovering alcoholic about staying sober and helps support them when they're having a hard time, kind of like a mentor. Dad has been through a few sponsors.

"Actually, I was thinking about asking Jack to be my sponsor again. You girls remember Jack, don't you?"

"Yeah," recalls Violet. *Jack's a good guy. Although he doesn't exactly have his life together, either.* "Does he still live with his mom?"

Donna laughs. "I think so. Probably still trying to find a way to get rich quick, too."

Violet notices Maggie trying to catch her eye, and looks back at her knowingly. She can see the hurt in Maggie's gaze. Jack may be a good guy, but he's not going to help Dad get straight. It hurts Violet to see Maggie hurt. Wanting to divert Maggie's attention, she deliberately turns and looks toward the living room, where the t.v. is. "So did you guys already rent a movie, or what?"

"We thought we'd go pick up some ice cream and rent a couple flicks while we're out," Dad says. "Let you girls pick what you want."

Maggie gets up and begins clearing dishes. Violet looks to Dad and Donna for direction, and since they are still sitting back in their chairs, Violet stays put too. "You guys can go," states Maggie stiffly. "I'll get this stuff cleaned up while you're gone."

Oh, come on Mag. Can't you just relax and enjoy yourself? Dad's fine right now. He's not drunk. We're here together. Let's have fun!

"Oh, no," Donna says, pulling out a pack of cigarettes and a lighter from her jeans pocket. She used to smoke in the house, but now she always goes out back. "You all go on and I'll clean up in a minute." She looks to Dad, "bring me back some Rocky Road."

Maggie continues to gather dishes and scrape plates into the garbage. All the pots and pans are still dirty too. "You guys cooked. I can clean up," she replies.

Uggh, I guess I need to clean too. Violet sits a little longer, too stuffed to move. Maggie's voice brings her out of the food coma she was about to fall into. "Violet, since I cleared the table, can you empty the dishwasher and take out the garbage?"

She looks at her sister for a moment before getting up. *So much for us going out for ice-cream while Donna cleans up.* "Yup," she says obediently. *Oh well. At least Donna won't have to do it.*

"I'll go get my keys," says Dad, pushing his chair back from the table and heading through the living room toward the stairs at the front of the house.

Donna heads toward the back door. "Thanks for doing that, girls. Don't touch the stuff on the stove, though. We didn't ask you over here to do chores. I want you to go have a good time with your Dad."

As Violet pulls clean glasses off the top rack of the dishwasher, she thinks about her secret admirer. The note's still tucked away in her book-bag, because every time she thinks of it she's either in class or with her friends, and she's still not ready to let anyone else in on it. She doesn't know if it's a prank or for real, and it's kind of nice to think that somebody at school has a secret crush on her. Thinks she's "awesome" and "super hot." Just as she starts to smile, recalling those words, doubt creeps in. *It's gotta be a prank. Who sends secret admirer notes?* But thinking about it that way's no fun. Inside her head, she sings to herself, *I have a secret admirer.*

9

Rachel is tense as she pulls out of the driveway. She was supposed to meet Jackie, Michelle, and Stephanie for sushi downtown at seven, and here it is 6:45 and she's just leaving her house. After a couple of bad months, David is back on the wagon and calling the girls again. *It's amazing how obvious it is when he's drinking and when he's sober.* He even offered to pick Violet up from rehearsal today, but Rachel already had it on her schedule and it seemed easier to just do it herself than to try and make arrangements with him. Had she known Violet was going to offer rides home to half the cast, she might have chosen differently. She barely had time to do her online bill pay before hopping back in the car. *That girl can be so damned selfish.* She feels her blood pressure rise a notch, and reminds herself that she'll have a nice glass of wine in a minute and she won't have to think about home, or work, or kids for a little while. She inhales deeply through her nose, blowing the breath out through pursed lips. *At least traffic doesn't look too bad*, she thinks as she pulls out onto the four lane road.

Thanksgiving is this Thursday. Rachel is having her parents over for dinner, and Violet has invited her friend Cecilia. *Sweet girl.* Rachel's parents live about two hours away, but they don't visit very often and they never spend the night, despite Rachel's frequent invitations. Cecilia, on the other hand, has had several holiday dinners with the Sanders over the years. She lives with her mother in a small, ranch-style house not far from

Rachel and the girls. Her mother works long hours in a diner and doesn't seem to do much for the holidays. She speaks very little English, but she always checks up on Cecilia to make sure she is where she says she's going to be, and to thank Rachel for having her. *I like that. Good family.* Rachel gets frustrated with Violet's friend Tonya, because she seems to have everything handed to her on a platter. Rachel gives Violet an allowance, but it's limited. Hanging out with Cecilia, who gets her spending money from what she saved with a summer job, is a reality check for Violet. Rachel has invited Cecilia's mother to come over for Thanksgiving dessert along with some neighbors and other friends, but she's unlikely to come.

Rachel has to drive around the block a couple of times before she finds a parking spot near the restaurant. *I should have called someone and told them to order me a drink!* She buttons her long, cream, fitted overcoat up as she climbs out of her car into the cold night. It's dark and wet out, with a misty drizzle. Boot heels click on the pavement, announcing her presence to the quiet street. The small city streets are never terribly crowded on a Monday night, but it seems especially quiet tonight. *Winter.* Her brow creases as she looks around at the shops, thinking about all the holiday shopping and shoppers she'll have to deal with soon.

When she gets to the restaurant, the ladies are already seated at their favorite table in the back. Rachel recalls bringing the girls here last Spring to celebrate Easter early because they were spending the holiday at David's parents' house. They had sat at this table then, but it didn't make for a pleasant evening. Violet was in one of her moods. It's a low table surrounded by benches sunken into the floor, so it has the feel of a traditional Japanese dining experience, without the discomfort of folding up your legs to sit on the floor. The experience is made more intimate still by sliding paper screens that turn it into a little private dining area.

Jackie sees Rachel and raises her hand to wave hello. Stephanie and Michelle wave as well, but are already deep in discussion. As Rachel pulls off her coat, Jackie gestures to the wine bottle on the table. "Wine, or are you going to have something else?"

"That looks good," Rachel replies, climbing down onto the bench.

As she sits, Jackie fills her in, "Stephanie and Rick are thinking of going on a cruise for their anniversary, and Ford wants them to leave him home alone."

Michelle turns to Rachel, "what do you think? Would you leave Maggie home alone if you were going away for a week?"

"Hmmm. You know if it were just Maggie, I guess I might. I mean, I would need to have somebody checking in on her, just to make sure she was okay, but I might." Rachel turns to look for the waiter.

Stephanie laughs across the table. "Yeah, I probably wouldn't think twice about leaving Maggie. Violet, on the other hand…" Jackie and Michelle join in on the laughter.

Michelle adds, "Rachel probably won't want to leave Violet alone when she's twenty-two, let alone eighteen." More laughter.

Rachel catches the waiter's eye and flags him down. She's glad to have an excuse not to engage in this discussion. *Okay, Violet may not always be the most responsible 16-year-old, but she's never done anything that bad.* "May I have a glass of water please, and a wine glass?" She turns her attention back to her friends. "So what are you thinking about leaving Ford?" *He's the one who got suspended two years ago for throwing things at his teacher when she turned to write on the board, isn't he?*

"I don't know," Michelle replies. "I have no reason not to trust him, but a week is a long time."

"Well, he'll be on his own all the time when he goes to college next year," reflects Jackie. Jackie's kids are only 4 and 7, so she tends to forget that adolescents are still children too.

"Don't remind me," Michelle groans. "But in the dorms, there are monitors to keep tabs on the kids."

"Yeah," Stephanie teases, "I know my dorm monitors kept great tabs on me. That's who went on beer runs for us!"

Rachel listens to her friends banter, and finds she can't quite get herself engaged. On the ride over, she looked forward to commiserating with the ladies about the frustrations of navigating motherhood, but now she finds herself feeling defensive about her kids rather than frustrated with them. Defensive of Violet, anyway.

As if on cue, Michelle asks her, "so what's going on with Violet's math class? Did she bring her grade up? Is she still saying it's the teacher's fault?"

At Violet's school, teachers are required to inform the parents any time a student's class average falls below a D. Rachel realizes that the last time she came out to dinner with the ladies, she had just finished talking to Violet about an email from her math teacher. Violet's grades have fluctuated over the years, but that was the first time Rachel had ever had to worry about one of her children failing a class. Violet had insisted it was the teachers fault, because he had lost her homework folder and put zeros on her progress report for several assignments that should have been 100s. Rachel hadn't bought the story, which is not only what she told Violet, but also what she had told these three women sitting here. In retrospect, it wouldn't be the first time a teacher messed up. "Actually, she's doing really well in all her classes. She brought her grade up to a B in math on her last report card, and I think she may get an A this quarter." *Shoot, I have no idea how she's doing in math this quarter. I need to check on that.*

"Good!" Michelle sounds positive, but Rachel is annoyed that she even asked the question. "And how are *your* classes going?"

This is a more pleasant topic of conversation. "Really good," Rachel says. "A couple more weeks and the semester will be over. Then one more semester, and I'm done!" Rachel is proud of her accomplishments. Her friends are all working mothers, but none of them seem to take their jobs too seriously. They have jobs, whereas as Rachel has a career.

"I remember how crazy you were during tax season last year, doing school and work at the same time." Stephanie comments. "You can't be looking forward to that..."

"You know, it's hard, but I don't really mind. It goes so quickly when you're busy. I don't know. I mean I'm not looking forward to it, but I don't mind." *If that's what I have to do to be successful, then that's what I'm going to do.* "Anyway, that's how I can afford to be a single mom and still have nights like this," she says proudly.

The ladies spend the rest of the evening talking about work, the holidays, vacations, husbands, and kids. Although Rachel has a couple of men that she has dated on and off over the years, she's never had a serious relationship since David, and she doesn't consider her love life a topic for conversation over dinner. Years ago, her friends would bring it up, asking questions and trying to play matchmaker, but they have since learned that the subject is fairly off limits. Michelle and Jackie are still with their first husbands, and Stephanie was only divorced for about a year and a half before she married again.

Rachel is the first to decline dessert when the waiter clears away their dinner plates. Normally she would at least have a coffee, but tonight she feels tired. Even more tired than usual. It's hard to relax with friends when there's work sitting on her desk undone, a school project to finish before finals, and a major holiday to prepare for. She hopes her friends will take the hint, and feels herself breathe a sigh of relief when everybody asks for their checks.

10

Violet is looking forward to the weekend. Chemistry has been really hard this semester, and much as she hates to admit it, she knows she can't get any more bad grades if she wants to get into a good college. She's been working her butt off to stay on top of her classes, exceed expectations in her role in Grease, and keep her social life moving. It's hard to stay focused on school, though, when she knows this weekend's gonna be slamming. Four full days with no school, and no one has anywhere they have to be. It's the best thing about the holidays.

Violet slaps her math textbook closed with a satisfactory thwack and shoves her school stuff off her bed. *Homework done, thank you!* She checks her watch: 8 o'clock. *I'm hungry.* Mom's out for the evening, so Violet's on her own for supper. Maggie was already eating a sandwich when Violet got home from rehearsal. *What should I eat?* she ponders. *Ramen Noodles. Yum!!!* She grabs her phone off the bed and skips down to the kitchen. *Why hasn't my baby texted me? I'll call him in a sec.*

In the kitchen, Violet gets water on the stove to boil before she dials Desmond's number. He sounds groggy when he answers. "What's wrong with my boo?" she queries sympathetically.

"Hey, babe. I'm just stressed. I feel like I spent all weekend working on college apps, and I still have so much to do. I keep trying to start my essay, but it just sounds stupid. I don't know what to write."

"Awww, baby," Violet coos. She is much too happy to have her man sounding so down. "Your essay's gonna be awesome. Write about me!" She hears him chuckle on the other end of the line, but he's not turning around as quickly as she'd like. They chat a few more minutes, and by the time she's got her Ramen Noodles served, she's made up her mind. "You're getting way too stressed about this. I can't have my boo feeling bad when we have a holiday weekend coming up, and everybody's supposed to be in a party head." Violet beams just thinking about it. "Go get in your car and come over here. You need some company." She sits at the island to eat.

"I would love to, hon, but I really need to get this stuff done."

"No," she insists. "You can't write an essay when you feel like crap. You're coming over here. You've got twenty minutes."

"Aright." She can practically hear him relax as he agrees to see her. "But be ready. We're going for a ride."

"I'll be ready," she replies cheerfully. "Hurry up."

Violet slurps her noodles quickly down. *I gotta see how I look before he gets here.* The better she feels, the more she cares about how she looks. She rinses her bowl and leaves it in the sink to run upstairs. She's wearing jeans, sneakers, a fitted t-shirt, and a hoody. It's not fancy, but it'll do. The important thing is how her face looks. She jets into the bathroom to check. She didn't wear any makeup today, and her hair's looking kind of raggedy, so she runs a brush through it and puts it up in a ponytail. *That works.* She gives her face a quick wash in the sink and slaps on some light eye makeup and lip gloss. *Gorgeous.* She heads back downstairs to wait for Desmond, who arrives a few minutes later. She is out the front door before he even makes it all the way up the driveway.

While Violet's mood has improved even further since she realized Desmond was coming over, his seems to have slumped since they last talked on the phone. He leans over to kiss her when she climbs into the car, but it's a weak kiss, just a formality. "Tell me about it," Violet urges. She doesn't want him to bring her mood down, but she's not gonna make him act cheerful if that's not how he's really feeling. They talk for a little while about Desmond's difficulty with getting all his work done and formulating an essay for his college applications. Violet listens attentively, offering him support where he needs it and advice where he wants it. By the time they make it to the other side of Franklin, Desmond has forgotten his difficulties and is laughing easily.

"I told you, you can't stress it. You work your ass off, everybody loves you, you'll be fine. We'll work on your essay this weekend."

"Come here." Desmond reaches his right hand behind Violet's back and pulls her over toward him. The center console digs into her side a little, but she doesn't care. She's happy that Desmond's happy. He kisses the top of her head and runs his fingers over her hair as he drives. "I think we need to pull over," he says a few minutes later.

"Me too," Violet agrees. Her head is resting on his shoulder, and she can smell his cologne. Desmond may be the only guy she knows that can wear cologne without suffocating everybody within fifty feet. She tilts her head back to kiss his neck, breathing in his scent. Violet was already having a good day, but being alone with Desmond now, being able to hear him, taste him, smell him, feel him is like winning a tropical vacation, then being told you won a million dollars too. She feels exhilarated and utterly content.

Desmond manages to bend his head down and kiss her deeply for a moment. She's been wanting to fool around with him all night, and he's going to make sure she gets her wish. He drives to a dark, sparsely populated residential street where he and Violet have hung out before. He knows it cause he used to have a friend who lived around here. He parks at the end of the road and turns his car off, extinguishing his lights with it. "It's gonna get cold," he warns her, one hand on her waist and the other on her cheek, running a thumb over her lower lip.

"I don't care," she assures him, and they lose themselves in each other for just a little while.

■ ■ ■

Rachel arrives home to a quiet house, and immediately goes on the alert. It's only 10 o'clock, and the girls should still be up and about. She hangs her coat up carefully in the front hall closet and pauses at the bottom of the stairs on the way to the kitchen. "HELLO?" she calls out. No answer. She takes a few steps up the stairs and calls out again, "MAGGIE?"

"Hi Mom!" Maggie calls as a bedroom door opens upstairs. Maggie appears at the top of the stairs moments later. "How was dinner?"

"It was nice." Rachel doesn't continue up the stairs, but stands where she is with one hand on the rail. "Where's Violet?" A car door slams outside.

"Desmond came and got her. That's probably her getting back. I told her she shouldn't go without your permission."

"Where did they go?"

"I don't know. I think she said they were just going for a ride or something."

Rachel is about to speak when the front door opens behind her. She turns around to see her daughter standing in the doorway, just registering that her mother is home.

"Hi Mom! You're home early!" Violet remarks, shutting the front door.

"Lock the door." Violet turns and does so, beginning to realize that Mom is not pleased about something. Rachel is terse: "Where were you?"

"I just went for a ride with Desmond. He was stressing out about college apps, and I told him to come get me so he could think about something else for awhile. Is that okay?"

Rachel's mind goes back to the comments about her daughter over dinner. Her friends see Violet as irresponsible, untrustworthy, manipulative. *You know you're not allowed out this late on a school night, especially without me knowing.* "Well, I don't know. Has it ever been okay for you to be out at 10 o'clock on a school night?"

"Yeeeeaaaaah," Violet responds cautiously. "I was out with Cecilia past ten last week when we had that science project due."

Rachel walks down the steps and brings herself face to face with Violet. "That was three weeks ago, and you were out past ten because you were working on something for school, AND I gave you permission to go out that night."

The temperature in the hallway rises. Violet clenches her fists at her sides. "Well, I'm SORRY. You didn't say I needed permission to go for a ride around the NEIGHBORHOOD, with my boyfriend who I've been with for a YEAR, who happened to NEED me tonight!" Violet moves to walk around her mother, but Rachel blocks her path.

"You're *sixteen* years old, Violet. You are not an adult, and you don't get to make adult decisions." Rachel's voice is firm and commanding. She doesn't yell... she doesn't have to. "If your boyfriend *needs* someone, he has parents he can talk to, or he can call you on the phone. I *know* Desmond doesn't expect you to be able to leave the house whenever you feel like it."

"Yeah, Mom. Desmond can talk to his *parents*, just like I can talk to *you*, right?" Violet has lowered her voice a decibel or two, but she is still loud, and her words fairly explode with sarcasm.

"Yes," Rachel demands, "you *can* talk to me. If you would talk to *me* a little more instead of being so caught up in how *you* think things are supposed to be done, you might actually learn how to *make* these kinds of decisions." She stares hard at Violet, willing her to listen, but Violet hears only the ice in her tone and the criticism in her words.

"Mom, I don't want to talk about this. I did what I felt I had to do. I'm sorry it didn't *please* you." *GOD, she's such a bitch. LEAVE me ALONE.* All the joy Violet had been feeling when she was with Desmond is suddenly snatched away, leaving a dangerous void, a soup of uncertainty and anxiousness.

Rachel laughs snidely. "You did what you had to do. Well you can do what you have to do in your room for the rest of this week. And I may need to rethink letting your friends come over for Thanksgiving."

Violet feels fury explode in her core. The one thing she was looking forward to, squashed before her very eyes. "You're a fucking BITCH!" she wails, turning and smashing into the front door as she tries to open it.

Rachel stands stunned for a moment as she watches her daughter struggle with the lock, then swing the front door wide. Violet has never, ever spoken to her mother that way before. Attitude, yes, but 'fucking bitch?' Within seconds, Rachel's adrenaline kicks in and the fight or flight instinct takes over. It doesn't tell her to flee. Rachel shouts Violet's name as she lunges forward and grabs her by the back of the hair, yanking her violently back. Violet feels herself being propelled backward, and turns her body to catch her fall. Rachel jumps back as she sees Violet fall hard at her feet, and finds herself once again stunned into stillness, evidence of her anger hanging in strands from her trembling hand.

Responding to her own instincts, Violet twirls around and jumps up, her body a tank at the ready. "I FUCKING HATE YOU!" Violet's hair is sticking out at all angles, and her eyes are dark with rage. "DON'T EVER FUCKING TOUCH ME AGAIN!"

Rachel is as still as a statue, eyes wide and lips parted in surprise. Violet's shoulders rise and fall, chest expanding powerfully as she tries to gain control of her breath. She stands glaring at her mother for a moment, then turns and walks swiftly out the front door, leaving it open behind her.

Rachel doesn't stir for several minutes, trying to make sense of what just happened. She looks up when she becomes aware of movement in the upstairs hallway. It is Maggie, just now abandoning her station at the top of the stairs. She was there the whole time. In the stillness, Rachel recalls hearing Maggie call out when she went after Violet. Now Maggie is silent, just another retreating body.

Rachel will reside in silence for several hours tonight. She continues the journey to the kitchen that she started... *when was that?* She looks at her watch: 10:15. *That was 15 minutes ago?* It is almost unbelievable. She sits at the table, hands folded on the hard surface, pensive. She reviews the sequence of events in her mind. It doesn't make sense. She goes over it again and again, but it never becomes clearer. There is no more sound from Maggie tonight. Several hours later, Rachel hears the front door open and footsteps going up the stairs. She looks at her watch, but doesn't register the time. She makes a mug of tea, but doesn't drink it. She gets out her laptop, but never turns it on. At 3:23, she carries her body up to the bedroom and takes off her boots, blouse, and slacks, dropping them on the floor where she stands. She climbs on the bed and lies on top of the covers in her bra and panties, staring at the ceiling. She listens to the silence, wondering vaguely if this is all real. The silence screams around her, echoing in her head. At 4:41, somehow, she sleeps.

11

When Violet walks out of the house after fighting with Rachel, she gets as far as the end of the driveway before she pulls out her phone to text Desmond. She doesn't even slow her pace as she furiously types:

i need u. can u com bak?

Her feet take her down the pavement in the general direction of Littleleaf Elementary. It is cold out, and windy. Her phone buzzes in her hand, and she looks at the screen:

lol. i need u 2, but i got skool tomoro. get som sleep boo. luv u!!!

Oh my God, he doesn't get it...

im serius. i need u. plz com get me.

Violet has made it two blocks, still headed toward the school. It is starting to drizzle steadily. She sees herself on the playground, and decides she'll head that way, but not stop there. Her phone buzzes again:

did somtin hapn?

Aaaagh, just come or don't come! She keeps walking. The rain is beginning to soak through her hair and she feels the coldness of it on her scalp. Her fingers are wet. She puts her phone in her sweatshirt pocket to wipe her hands on her jeans before taking it back out and typing:

if u cant com, i undrstand. just wanted to talk to u.

Water begins to puddle on the street, splashing as she trudges on. She reaches the school property and steps into the wet grass, neither slowing nor changing her course. The dark and the cold and the wet seem to envelope Violet, cloaking her from the rest of the world. She feels angry and alone, yet powerful. Untouchable. She hears her phone ring once, twice. She continues to walk, then realizes he may have decided to come, and she answers it. "Hello?"

Desmond's voice is cautiously solicitous. The connection is fuzzy. "Vi, where are you?"

Something about hearing his voice seems to break the spell. She stops walking. Violet suddenly finds herself caught in the open, a wet blob in an open field trying not to let her phone get wet. "At the school."

"Do you want me to come get you?"

"Yeah." Defeated. She feels like she should cry now, but the tears don't come. She turns and heads back toward the street and the tree line along the edge of the property.

"Stay there, babe. Are you getting wet?"

"Yeah." She feels her muscles loosen slightly. Her neck and the back of her head begin to ache. The cold creeps in like a ghost. She is shivering. "I'm cold." Water drips down her hand and onto her phone as she reaches the shelter of a tree. She leans against the wide trunk with her right shoulder as she runs the fingers of her left hand over the deep, rough grooves.

"Why don't you run back home and I'll meet you there?"

"No. Just come here. I'll see you in a minute, okay?"

"Well, do you wanna stay on the phone?"

"No." Violet doesn't want to stay on the phone. She doesn't want to stay on the earth. She wants to disappear. It occurs to her that Mom hasn't called. No one is on the street. Mom could have come after her, but she didn't. "Just come on." Her voice is soft, worn. "I'll see you in a second." She hangs up without waiting for a response. She lays her forehead on the tree trunk, rainwater dripping from her hair, running down her nose and over her lips. She presses her left palm against the hard grain and breathes in the scent of damp wood. *I wish I could sink right into this tree.* One teardrop works its way out of her right eye, and then she starts. No sound, no sobbing, just thick tears tracing the course of her pain. She turns her back to the tree and leans against it, waiting to see Desmond's headlights in the night.

12

It is Thursday morning. Thanksgiving. Violet lounges in bed, not quite ready to face the day. It has been a weird week. Violet hung out with Desmond until two in the morning Monday night. When she told him what happened, instead of taking her side, he was like, "wow, you guys really had it out." *Hello? We had it out? She freaking attacked me!* Violet shut down after that. He kept trying to hug her and kiss her, but she just wasn't into it. She didn't want his comfort after that. It seemed fake... contrived. Honestly, it felt like he wanted Violet to hurry up and feel better so he could get home and go to bed.

She has pretty much ignored Mom all week. Mom's been talking to her a little, but Violet just gives one word answers and stuff. She still hasn't apologized for Monday. Hasn't even mentioned it. It had been such a good day, and Mom smashed it in an instant. Violet's head is still a little sore in one spot from where her mother yanked her hair. *She probably doesn't even think she did anything wrong.* She rolls over in bed and stares out the window. Mom gets mad because she always leaves the curtains open, but she can't help it. She likes to see the moon at night, and watch the clouds float by in the morning.

Violet hasn't told anybody about her secret admirer notes. There was another one a couple of weeks ago. She was having a bad day at school, which she apparently didn't hide very well, because when she went to her locker after lunch there was a handwritten note stuck inside:

I hate to see you frown… hope this note turns it upside down!
looking at you makes me smile… See! I told you I'd be around awhile.
Still waiting patiently,
S.A. :)

It did make her smile, and it continues to. The notes have moved into her desk drawer. The first text really seemed like a prank, but this one's too sweet to be a prank. She has asked herself if it's messed up to keep these when she has a boyfriend, but since S.A. doesn't know she's kept them, and she doesn't even know who S.A. is, it seems innocent enough.

Violet rolls out of bed, thinking about her mother. *She's been nice to me all week. Well, starting Tuesday. Maybe if I say sorry first, she'll say sorry too.* She heads downstairs in her t-shirt and pajama pants and stops outside the kitchen. She can hear Mom and Maggie in there, already preparing food for dinner. Maggie sounds cheerful, "Michael's going to bring some of that cinnamon coffee his mom gets to have with dessert. It'll go good with this apple cake, don't you think?" Michael and Maggie have been dating for about six months.

"That sounds delicious." Mom sounds distracted, but doesn't she always?

Violet meanders into the kitchen. "Mornin!" She heads to the cabinet and pulls out a sauce pan. There are two cookie sheets laid across the cook-top, and she slides one over to make room for her pan before turning and opening the fridge. "Where's the milk? You guys want some hot chocolate?"

"Good morning," Mom responds, reaching into the turkey to pull out the neck. "It's on the counter behind you."

Maggie doesn't stop what she's doing either. She picks up her metal bowl and tilts it toward a white ceramic dish, using a spatula to scrape the sides. "Violet, seriously, do you have to make hot chocolate right now?"

Ummm, no? Maggie leaves the pan on the stovetop, but poors herself a glass of cold milk instead. "What can I do?"

Mom stops, looks at her, and smiles. "Do you want to start peeling potatoes?"

Well, not really, but okay. "Sure!"

Violet looks around for potatoes, and her mom helps her out. "They're in the pantry."

Nobody speaks for several minutes as they each focus on their individual tasks. It occurs to Violet that Maggie was perfectly content to have their mother all to herself. *Too bad, Sister. Okay, things are good so far. Mom's leaving me alone. Cecilia, Grammy, and Grandpa are coming over in a couple hours, then Desmond, Tonya, and Cam are coming over for dessert. Then after that, party tonight! Shit, I haven't told Mom yet.* Violet looks around the kitchen. Mom has gotten the turkey all cleaned up and is prepping it with herbs. Maggie has put her cake into the oven and is putting together the ingredients for a cheesecake. *I wish Maggie would get outta here so I could talk to Mom.* "So who's coming over for dessert?"

Mom chops fresh rosemary for the turkey. "Well, I guess you girls are having your boyfriends. Is Tonya coming?"

"I think so. And I think Cam's gonna stop by, Cecilia's boyfriend."

"So Tonya, Cam, Stephanie, Rick, and Ford, the Jacobsons, Louise and Ralph, and a couple of other people may be coming. Sylvia needed to see how things go at her house, and I invited a couple of people from school who were also going to play it by ear."

"What about the Harrises?" Violet likes their daughter, Rebecca. She plays drums in a band, and has taught Violet a lot about the music business.

"They're actually having Thanksgiving in New York. Rebecca has a show, so Stephanie and Rob decided to go up there and make a long weekend of it."

Maggie is working on the graham cracker crust for her cheesecake. "That sounds like fun."

"Yeah, I would love to do something like that," Violet thinks aloud. "Would you ever wanna do something like that Mom?"

"Oh, I don't know. I really enjoy the opportunity to have everybody over here."

"Yeah," Maggie adds. "A trip to New York sounds nice, but not for a holiday. It wouldn't feel right."

"That's right," jokes Violet, "for you guys, it's not a holiday unless it comes with two days of prep work and ten hours of clean-up afterwards." Violet is still working on getting the potatoes peeled. Out of the blue, a damp, wadded up paper towel comes flying at her. It bounces off her forehead and onto the floor. "Maggie!" she laughs, throwing it back at her.

"Behave," Maggie kids her as she crosses the room to check the oven. "Mom, can I put the cheesecake in with the apple cake?"

"Let the apple cake go another fifteen minutes, and then you can put the cheesecake in. Is the cheesecake ready?" Mom is slathering garlic butter onto the turkey now, inside, under the skin, everywhere. The smell of baked apples has begun to fill the kitchen.

"I just need to pour the batter in," answers Maggie, positioning the springform pan so that she won't spill.

"Well, go ahead and get that ready to go, then why don't you go take your shower? I can get everything into the oven, and that way you'll be ready to help again when it's time to work on the appetizers."

Maggie shakes the pan to even out the batter, then slides it into the center of the island to wait. "Okay." She carries her dirty dishes to the sink, addressing Violet as she goes, "Vi, since you just got here, will you wash the dishes when you're done with the potatoes?"

Fun. You get to bake cakes, and I get to be the dishwasher. Just what I wanted! Violet needs to talk to Mom, and she doesn't want to ruin the mood, so she agrees. She bides her time peeling potatoes for the next several minutes as Mom finishes dressing the turkey. When Mom begins to pull carrots and onions and celery out of the fridge, Violet decides it's time. "Mom, I'm sorry for what I said on Monday. I shouldn't have disrespected you like that."

Mom lays her vegetables on the counter and rinses the cutting board she had used for her herbs. She doesn't respond right away. She lays a celery stalk on the cutting board and cuts it into three long spears, then reaches for another to do the same. "Violet, I get frustrated with you because I worry about you. You're a child, and it's my job to set boundaries for you. I need you to understand that. I need to know that when I tell you to do something, I can trust you to do it." Mom gathers her celery spears and begins chopping them into tiny pieces. These will go into the stuffing.

Mom did not provide the response she was looking for. She wants to protest. *You never told me I had a curfew! You can't say I don't listen when you never told me to begin with!* She gives herself a minute to process the situation. Violet is down to her last two potatoes. Peeling is the hard part. When she's done, she'll cut each one into large chunks to be boiled for mashed potatoes. *I don't wanna fight with her. I'm trying to make things better. And I wanna go to this party tonight.* "Sorry." *It's all she can come up with. If Mom's not gonna meet me halfway, then who cares? She's obviously not sorry for grabbing me.*

"Let's just try not to let anything like that happen again. I shouldn't have lost control."

Finally! And you're sorry, right? "Okay. And I'm sorry I didn't tell you I was going out."

"It's over now. Let's just enjoy the day." Chop, chop, chop.

Right. Enjoy the day. Violet is aggravated, but she doesn't want to be. *It doesn't matter. She probably won't do it again. Just act like you respect her, and every-thing will be fine. Friends are coming over. Long weekend. No worries.* "Hey, is it okay if some of us go out after dessert tonight?"

"Who and where?"

"Well, all of us. I mean, me, Desmond, Cecilia, Cam, Tonya. One of Desmond's friends is having some people over." *Paaaaartyyyyyyy!*

"Is Desmond driving?"

Haha. Mom thinks Desmond can do no wrong. "Yup. It's one of his friends from school." *Which means she also thinks his friends can do no wrong.*

"Okay, but I want you home by 2:00 at the latest."

"Sounds good! Thanks, Mom." Violet's friends' parents would prob-ably ask about alcohol at the party, but Rachel doesn't think in those terms. *Good kids don't drink. Sometimes it's nice having a mom that knows nothing about my life.* Violet smiles contently.

13

Everybody is stuffed. Even Cecilia, who is not known for overdoing it. Desmond was polite enough to invite Maggie, Michael, and Ford to the party, but *thank God they said no. Not that there's anything wrong with them; I just don't wanna have to worry about my business getting back to Mom.* They stayed in the living room hanging with the adults, while Violet brought Cecilia, Cam, Desmond, and Tonya up to her room.

"Let's go get ready," Cecilia suggests. She is sitting on the bed, flipping through a magazine, with Tonya laid out beside her. By "get ready," she means go to the bathroom, fix her hair, and clean up her makeup.

Desmond is sitting on the desk, Cam is on the floor leaning against the bed, and Violet has been in and out of the closet looking for something to wear. "Uggh, I hate cold weather. And I hate trying to find something to wear after I just ate 10 pounds of turkey."

"Wear the blue," Tonya says, jumping up from the bed. "It makes your skin look less pasty." She grabs the yellow sweater off the chair and holds it up to her chest. "I think I might wear this one."

"You look good in both, Vi." Cecilia is getting up too. "Wear what feels comfortable. Tonya, let her decide what she wants to wear before you start raiding her clothes."

"She doesn't care," Tonya retorts, pulling the sweater on and buttoning it up the front. "You gonna wear this or that?"

"I'll wear this one." Violet winks at Desmond. "Gotta keep that pasty skin under control. I'm going to the bathroom," she calls over her shoulder as she heads out into the hall. Cecilia and Tonya follow.

In the bathroom, Cecilia plops her purse on the counter and pulls out a comb, hair mousse, powder, eyeshadow, eyeliner, and lip gloss. Violet already has her brush in her hand. She pauses to look over at Cecilia's stash. *That's a lot of freaking beauty supplies.* "Are you gonna use all that?"

"I don't know. I just figured I'd get it all out in case. You want me to do your makeup?"

Yes!

"Oooh, yes!" squeals Tonya. She grabs Violet and directs her toward the toilet. "Sit, sit."

Uhhh, no. "I'm good. I'm just gonna put some eyeliner and mascara on." *I want Cecilia to do my makeup, not crazy Tonya.*

"Oh, come on! Do something different for Desmond. We'll do the sexy, smoky look," Tonya urges.

"How bout you put on the sexy, smoky look, and I'll stick to the I'm Freaking Amazing Just the Way I Am look?" challenges Violet lightly.

"Put on your eyeliner and mascara," Cecilia directs, "and I'll add a little color to highlight your eyes and cheekbones. Do you have blush?"

Tonya is back in the drawer. "Here's some!"

"That's Maggie's." Violet takes it and closes it back in the drawer. "I have some in here," she pulls open a second drawer and takes out her makeup bag. She has about three things in it.

Cecilia is busy working on her own makeup, smudging dark eyeshadow into the crease of her eyelid. When she's done, the guys won't even notice a difference, but Tonya and Violet see it.

"You're gorgeous," Violet smiles at her.

"I know," Cecilia jokes with a straight face. "Tough to be me. Do you have baby oil?"

"Of course," Violet pulls it out from under the sink and lets a few drop fall into her palm, then passes the bottle to Cecilia. She rubs her palms together and smoothes the oil over her hair, focusing on the tips. Cecilia does the same with her curls, scrunching it in.

"So who's gonna be at this party?" asks Tonya, brushing Cecilia's powder over her face. It's a little dark for her skin tone, but Tonya will rub it in, make it work. Tonya has a knack for making things work.

"I don't know," Violets shrugs. "St. Frances kids."

"Sweet. I need to meet some new people."

"What's going on with you and Marcus? Did you tell him to come?" Violet wonders. *Please say no.*

"Uck, Marcus. I'm over him. You remember that night we were all doing coke at Desmond's?"

Shut up, Tonya. Cecilia doesn't even know about that. But Cecilia doesn't look surprised. *Does Cecilia know? And we weren't 'all doing coke.'* "You mean the night you and Marcus did coke, and laced the blunt for the rest of us?"

"Whatever. I thought that was just a one time thing, but turns out Marcus does coke, like, all the time. I just couldn't take it anymore. I'm not trying to hook up with a drug addict."

"Good for you," Cecilia says. "You don't need that crap."

"I know, right? I did so much coke when I was with him. I'm over it. I don't even wanna do pills anymore." Tonya is back in Maggie's drawer, sorting through her things.

Violet looks at her disapprovingly, but lets it go. *What Maggie doesn't know won't hurt her.* She has finished with her eyes and turns to Cecilia, blush in hand. "Uhhh, Tonya, didn't you just pop a pill last Sunday with Teah?"

"One pill. I didn't, like, get fucked up or anything. Do you guys have any perfume?" She sits down on the edge of the bathtub, looking at Violet inquisitively.

"I don't know. I might have some in my room." Violet is leaned up with her left hip against the counter while Cecilia applies color to her cheeks and eyes.

"Perfect." Cecilia turns Violet's chin to show her in the mirror.

"Thanks girl. We ready?"

"Good to go," says Cecilia, returning her eyeshadow to her purse.

"Ready and willing!" declares Tonya, as she pops up and leads the pack back to the bedroom.

■ ■ ■

The party turns out to be more fun than Violet has had in awhile. People are drinking, but hardly anybody's stupid drunk. There are games in the basement, poker, and darts, and foosball, and a DJ in the living room with the furniture pulled out of the way for a dance floor. Violet had one wine cooler when they first got here, but that was two hours ago and she hasn't wanted anything since. She and Tonya and Cecilia are dancing around like 12 year olds, and it is FUN. Tonya jumps into the middle of the dance floor and starts doing the robot in front of some guy she never met before. He looks at her like she is crazy, and the three girls burst into giddy laughter. Violet sees Desmond, Cam, and Jaden looking at them skeptically from a few feet away, and that sends her off into another wave of giggles. She stumbles off the dance floor and falls against the wall, laughing so hard her cheeks ache. Cecilia and Tonya practically fall on top of her, completely overcome by the silliness of it all. *I love these girls.* She hugs her friends. "I LOVE you guys!"

Tonya plants a kiss on Violet's cheek and bellows, "I LOVE YOU TOO!"

After several more minutes of laughter, prolonged by unprovoked giggle fits by one or another of the girls, they all finally calm down and begin to catch their breath. Violet laughed so hard she cried, and very nearly peed herself. *I am so happy right now.* The guys have wandered off somewhere, probably embarrassed to be associated with these three, but Violet doesn't care. "Let's go outside. I'm hot."

"I need to pee," Tonya protests.

"Me too," agrees Cecilia.

"Let's go," Violet consents, heading toward the hallway. "I think I saw a bathroom over here."

"I must look like a freak right now," Tonya says, falling in behind her. "Vi, you're all sweaty."

"Good," Violet throws back as she weaves her way through the crowded hall, "keeps the creeps away. Oh wait, I guess there's a line. Are you waiting?" she asks another girl, indicating the bathroom.

"No, but I think he is," she answers, pointing at someone standing outside the bathroom door.

"Thanks." She sidles up next to the boy and makes room for Tonya and Cecilia beside her. "I am having so much fun."

"I know, this is awesome. There are some hot guys here." Tonya looks down the hall, then turns back toward the short, thin guy standing outside the bathroom and laughs loudly. "Emphasis on the word *some*."

Cecilia shakes her head and Violet gives Tonya a meaningful glare, hoping the boy didn't catch Tonya's reference. Cecilia changes the subject, "it feels like the old days. Remember in middle school when we would go to a party and just be *stupid*, and have so much fun?"

"Oh my God, this does *not* feel like middle school," Violet counters, sliding closer to the bathroom when the guy in front of her goes in. "Elementary school, maybe. At middle school parties, we were all so worried about looking cool, I think we forgot to have a good time. Middle school was fun when we would all just get together and hang out. Like, go to the movies and stuff."

"That's true," Cecilia agrees. "And then when we got to high school, all anyone ever wanted to do was get drunk and high." She seems to realize what she's saying just as the words come out. The truth is, Tonya still gets drunk or high at most parties, and Violet's not much better.

Violet meets Cecilia's eyes and gives her a half smile. *God, I've been a shitty friend, haven't I?* Her mind turns to Desmond, and the bathroom door opens. The three girls walk in together and Cecilia locks the door behind them. *I wonder if Desmond feels like Cecilia. I should go find him after we're done.*

Tonya uses the facilities first. "Speaking of drunk and high, I need to go get a drink. Just because I'm done with drugs doesn't mean I can't still have fun!"

Dumbass. You are so oblivious. The girls play with their hair and makeup while each one takes a turn peeing.

"I still wanna get some fresh air after this," Cecilia says.

"Yeah, me too. You wanna see if the guys wanna come outside?" Violet asks Cecilia.

"Sure. Ready?" Cecilia checks with her friends before opening the bathroom door and heading back toward the living room.

"You guys don't want a drink?" Tonya asks, stopping outside the bathroom.

"I'm good," Cecilia answers.

"Me too," Violet adds. "Just meet us outside."

"Okey dokey!" Tonya turns her back on her friends and heads toward the kitchen.

Cecilia talks loudly so as to be heard over the music as she and Violet walk through the house, looking for Cam and Desmond. "She is so funny. You know she'll find a guy to talk to in like two seconds."

Funny. Violet looks at her friend. *You are so positive. What a good friend you are. You call it funny, I call it slutty. Oh well.* "Maybe they're downstairs."

"Come on." The girls slip down the stairs and see Desmond and Cam standing near the poker table. Jaden is playing with two other guys and a girl. There are a few other people standing around watching. *Why are you watching people play cards?* Violet looks over the spectators. *That seems so boring.* She slips easily into Desmond's arms and gives him a peck on the lips. "Hey babe. Miss me?"

He only gives her half his attention, still watching the poker players. "Of course I missed my boo."

She turns around and presses her back into Desmond's chest, his arms still encircling her. *Seriously, what are you looking at?* The players show their cards, and someone reaches out for the pile of chips in the center of the table. *Hmph. So anyway...* "Hey, you wanna come outside? Get some air?"

"Sure." He pulls his arms back and drops his hands down into hers, looking over at Cam and Cecilia. "You guys coming?"

They have apparently had a similar conversation, because they are already moving by the time Desmond shuts his lips. The group heads up the stairs and out the front door. They plant themselves on the large concrete landing at the bottom of the steps. It's a large house on a large lot, with one big tree in the front yard, and lots of small, young shrubs and trees around the foundation and out by the street. The music from inside is easily heard where they stand, along with a steady murmur of voices.

Cam stands furthest from the house, with his back to the street. He has his arm draped across Cecilia's shoulders. "Where's Tonya?"

Cecilia stands with her arms crossed, already feeling the chill. It's warm for a November night, probably 60 degrees out, but it still feels cold. "She went to get a drink. She might meet us out here."

Desmond is facing the street, leaning back against the railing. He draws Violet toward him and wraps both arms around her. She leans into him, body turned sideways toward her friends. His tone is matter-of-fact: "be okay with me if she keeps her ass inside."

"Desmond," Violet scolds. "What has she ever done to you?"

"She hasn't done anything to me. I just don't trust her. I honestly don't know how you two put up with her."

"You just can't get wrapped up in her shit," Cecilia explains. "She's not out to hurt anyone. And we've known her forever. I mean, if somebody really does me wrong, I'm not afraid to walk away, but Tonya's not like that. That thing with the coke was obnoxious, but that's just cause she doesn't think things through. You gotta look out for yourself when you're with her, and you'll be fine. She can be really fun to hang out with. And she needs good friends. She falls into a lot of shitty relationships, with guys *and* girls."

Obviously Cecilia knows about the cocaine. Who told her?

"Yeah," Desmond counters, "but at what point does she stop getting into those relationships, and start being accountable for her decisions?"

Did Cam know? Did Desmond tell him? When would Desmond have told him?

"I know," Cecilia maintains, "she makes bad choices. And at some point she's gonna have to learn to make better choices. I'm not stepping in to save her if she screws things up for herself, but I can still be an example for her of what a good friend is. She'll grow up eventually. I mean, I've done things to Cam that he didn't like, but he stuck around anyway, and I think we're closer because of it."

Did Tonya tell Cecilia?

Cam chuckles at this. "Cecilia, you've done stuff that I wasn't thrilled about, but you don't do the crazy shit Tonya does. I mean, I like Tonya, I'm glad you're friends with her, but I definitely think you needa watch your back with her too. And if you were any other girl, I probably wouldn't want you hanging with her at all."

Uh oh. Don't say that in front of Desmond. "She's not that bad," Violet jumps in. "Cecilia's right. We've been friends with her forever. We can't just turn our backs because she does a couple of stupid things. That's not what a true friend does. She's just going through a stage. She just told us tonight that she cut Marcus off cause he used too many drugs and she doesn't wanna do that anymore. And she apologized to me for putting stuff in the blunt without telling me." Violet didn't plan this lie in advance, but if she's trying to make Tonya look good, she's gonna have to embellish a little, *cause Tonya's not that good.*

"Really?" Desmond sounds genuinely surprised. "Huh." Thoughtful, chewing on this.

Damn, why did I just lie to him? "I know, right? She doesn't mean any harm. She's just immature. She's a good person at heart." Violet avoids Cecilia's gaze. Cecilia knows good and well that Tonya didn't apologize for lacing the pot.

The front door opens, and out walks Tonya. "Here they are!" she calls behind her. "Hey guys!" she skips down the steps, landing next to Violet and Desmond. "This is Josh, Franklin, and Tamika." She has a large, red, plastic cup in her hand, which she uses to gesture toward her friends. "This is Violet, Desmond, Cecilia, and Cam."

The tall guy with a big nose and curly, longish, black hair nods at Desmond. "Hey, dude."

"Hey, Franklin," Desmond replies. Then to Violet, "we're in economics together. Hey guys," he turns to Josh and Tamika, "I see you met Tonya."

"Oh," laughs Tonya. "I forgot, you would know these guys. But Josh, you said you don't go to St. Anthony's?"

"I graduated, silly." Josh is about Violet's height, with sandy brown hair and dark eyes. He walks down the steps to join the others. "I know Desmond. Good to see you, man." Josh reaches over to slap hands with Desmond.

"Yeah, man. You too. Where are you in school now?" Desmond asks.

Tonya walks around Josh and sits on the second step from the bottom.

"State. You figure out where you goin yet?"

"Nah. I'm workin on it, but I haven't made any decisions. It's crazy, man. I feel like I'm trying to make up my mind at 18-years-old about what the rest of my life is gonna be like… Makes me batty sometimes."

"No way, man. It's all good. You'll pick a good school. Don't stress about it."

"It's cold out here!" declares Tonya from behind Josh. He turns and looks down at her.

"Well, you're sitting on the concrete. Of course it's gonna be cold! Come on, let's go see what's goin on downstairs." Josh turns back to Desmond. "Good to see you man," then looks around at Violet, Cecilia, and Cam. "Hey, good meeting you all. We'll see you later."

"You too, man," Desmond responds as Josh turns away.

Tonya takes Josh's hand to pull her up. "See you inside!" She bounces up the steps. "It's way too cold out here."

When the door shuts and the four friends are alone outside again, Cecilia pipes up. "I think I'm ready to go inside too."

Violet grabs Desmond's hand. "Me too," she says, pulling him up the steps. "Let's go dance."

Desmond rolls his eyes, but doesn't offer any resistance. "How bout you dance, and I watch."

"Oh, come on!" Violet complains. "I wanna dance with *you*." She swings her hips to the music as she walks through the front door.

Just as they reach the living room, the rhythmic melody of a reggae jam kicks in. Desmond smiles and nods his head, hands on Violet's hips. "On second thought…" He pulls her close and they begin to move together. Good times.

14

Rehearsals for Grease are well under way. It turns out being a main character is totally different from being in the chorus. Every week Mr. Kettle, the director, gets harsher. And he's obsessed with the girl playing Sandy. Sarah sees it too. She got picked to play Cha Cha, which isn't as good as Violet's role, but still decent. Sandy is being played by Heather.

Heather was nice when rehearsals started, but the more Mr. Kettle compliments her and criticizes everybody else, the more condescending she becomes. Violet and Sarah stand in the wings watching her rehearse one of her scenes. Sarah didn't have to come last weekend, but it's the fourth consecutive Saturday Violet's had to be here. "God," Sarah whispers, "I'm getting so sick of listening to Mr. Kettle fawn over her. I mean, she's good, but she's not *that* good."

"I know," Violet agrees. "We're all working hard here. I was one of the first ones to get my lines memorized, and he hasn't even mentioned that. Heather still doesn't have all her scenes memorized."

"Seriously. I know she has a lot of lines, but still. The show's in two weeks."

Mr. Kettle calls out from the third row, where he always sits, "okay, let's move on to the next scene!"

The actors spread out on the stage, and Violet takes her place behind Heather. This is strictly a dance scene for Marty Maraschino, and it's the one Violet's been having the most trouble with. She tries to avoid Mr. Kettle's eyes as Mrs. Landron, the chorus teacher, plays the intro on the piano. *I have to get this right today.* She can't help but feel that Mr. Kettle's constant instruction is his way of telling her she sucks. *Why can't he ever say anything nice?* It's hard to concentrate on the dance when she's sure he's going to correct her any second. *At least Mrs. Landron is happy with me. Damn,* she scowls as she starts to turn the wrong way, but catches herself and falls in line with the other dancers.

The musical has been more draining than she could have imagined. Tons of people will see her perform. It's not like in middle school or the little recitals she's done where she practically knew everybody in the audience. If she screws up, half the school will see her do it, and that's all some of them will ever know her for. And worse, if she can't make Mr. Kettle happy, she won't get shit for a part in the school musical next year. It would kill her to be shoved back into the chorus her senior year. She couldn't stand it. Whenever Violet's had a hard time with her classes, she's been able to reason that *it's just one class; it's not the end of the world.* But for some reason, she can't convince herself of that with this show.

The cast manages to make it through the whole number without being stopped. Mr. Kettle doesn't comment until the music has ended. "Great job. Guys, make sure you're not crowding the ladies in the middle section. Violet, you had it perfect this week. Good work. We'll run through it one more time, and then let's try Scene Ten. We really need to get that cleaned up."

Really? Perfect? Sweet! It's probably not the first compliment Violet has gotten from Mr. Kettle, but it seems as if it is. She has a solo and some complicated harmonies in Scene Ten, and she decides to try and make it her best performance yet. They run through Scene Ten five times. Mr. Kettle doesn't really criticize Violet, but he doesn't have anything positive to say either. *Jerk. I knew it was too good to be true. I kicked butt in that song today, but you're too busy tearing everybody else apart to notice. God, I'm tired.*

After Scene Ten, Violet gets a 20 minute break while they work on one of the scenes with Sandy and Johnny. Sarah's done for the day, but Violet still has one more scene to rehearse after this. Sarah goes with her to the cafeteria to get a soda from the vending machine. A couple of the techie kids from the show are sitting in a back corner eating chips. "Hey guys!" Sarah calls when she sees them.

Oh, please don't go over there. Violet doesn't know them that well, and she just wants to relax for a little while. Unfortunately, that is exactly where Sarah's headed. Violet decides to go ahead and get her soda, hoping Sarah will just say a quick hello and come back. She can hear them chatting, but the voices in her head drown out what they're saying. *Just a couple more weeks til showtime. You need to keep your head up, Vi. You can rest later.* The soda can clanks through the machine and rolls out into the tray. She picks it up without turning around and walks to the cafeteria entrance, where she turns back and smiles a question at Sarah.

"Coming!" Sarah responds.

Phew. Vi smiles and waves at the others as Sarah tells them bye, but wanders into the hallway to wait while Sarah gets her drink. "Did you wanna stay with them?" Vi asks easily when Sarah joins her.

"Nah," Sarah responds. "I said I would have a drink with you, not with them. Let's go sit outside for a minute."

"Kay." They head back toward the front of the school and hang out for another ten minutes before Violet excuses herself to wait back in the theater for her next scene.

Violet stays home that night. She's disappointed when Desmond says he can't come over, but she still doesn't wanna hang with anybody else. She was in the mood to cuddle with him while she works on her lines. She thought she had them down pat, but she started screwing them up at the end of rehearsal today. Maggie's home too. *Maybe I'll ask her to run lines with me.* But instead, Violet falls fast asleep.

15

The gym is hot and stuffy, in spite of the cold outside. Violet, perched on the bottom row of the bleachers, holds the box still, afraid the faint rattle of its contents will echo uncontrollably in the big, empty space. It was in the pocket of her Pink Lady jacket, so it's gotta be someone in her classes *and* in the play. *Who would that be?* It's getting kind of freaky.

It's Friday evening, the week before Grease. Dress rehearsal. She has escaped alone to the gym for a few minutes to contemplate this latest gift. Her throat has been hurting for two days, and she woke up this morning with no voice. Mom doesn't even realize there's a problem. Violet wanted to tell her this morning, but she was gone before Violet got up, and when Violet called her, croaking at her through the phone, Mom just got mad cause she thought Violet's voice was hoarse from just waking up. So Violet didn't say anything. The director didn't help either when he was like, 'I'm sure you'll be fine by next week. Worst case, you've got an understudy.' *Thanks a freaking lot.* This is Violet's first big role in a school musical, and she is not going to miss out.

She looks at the top of the lozenge box for a minute before tearing it open. *I have a sore throat, may as well suck on a cough drop.* Cherry. *Not bad.* There was a post-it stuck to the box that said: *You'll be better by Monday —S.A. ;)* That note is in the garbage. *I gotta figure out what kinda freak is stalking me. This has gone a little beyond cute.* She goes through the cast in her head, but finds herself no closer to an answer. *I think I'm gonna have to bring the girls in on this. Ughh, I NEED MY THROAT TO GET BETTER!* She stuffs the box in her jeans and heads back to the auditorium.

■ ■ ■

Maggie drives Violet home Friday night. She has been driving Mom's car a lot lately, and Violet overheard them talking the other day about how to get Maggie a car of her own… *Lucky.* Violet had planned to go to Cecilia's after dress rehearsal, but she called earlier and told Cecilia she didn't feel like it. Too stressed and worried about not being able to sing.

She goes straight to her room when she gets out of the car and shuts herself in, locking the door. *Shit, I gotta wash this makeup off.* She drops her coat on the floor and heads to the bathroom. She closes the bathroom door, turns the tap water to hot, pulls off her shirt and unzips her jeans. *Why am I taking my clothes off? Screw it; I'll take a shower.* She turns off the water in the sink and turns on the water in the tub, as hot as it will go. She pushes her jeans down her thighs and puts her left foot on the cuff of her right jean leg to pull her right leg out as she unsnaps her bra. Bra on the floor, and she switches feet to get her left leg out of the jeans. There's no steam emanating from the tub, so she steps toward the mirror to examine her face. She runs her fingers across her forehead, looking for pimples, and is distracted by a couple of random hairs messing up her brow line. The air in the bathroom grows thick with moisture as she searches through her drawer for a tweezer. By the time she looks back at the mirror, it has developed a thin film of fog. She leans way forward and plucks the first hair with difficulty, then swipes her hand back and forth across the glass to clear things up before attacking the next culprit. *Damn eyebrow hairs.*

Violet drops her panties to her ankles, turns the knob for the showerhead, and closes the curtain. She has to turn the temperature way down before it is cool enough for her to get in. She stands in the middle of the stream for several minutes, eyes closed and arms resting at her side. She doesn't move until the water has thoroughly penetrated her thick hair and founds its way into all her crevices. *Aaaah.* Even her throat feels better.

Should I try a note? She parts her lips, then thinks better of it. *I'm not making a sound tonight. I'm gonna wake up in the morning, and I'll be good as new.* Shampoo. Conditioner. Face soap. Body wash. Another few minutes soaking in the spray. Turn shower off. Towel dry. Lotion, lotion, lotion. Towel one: turban. Towel two: wrap. Back to the bedroom.

Once in her pajamas, Violet presses her Ipod into the speaker and hits play. *Jeans... bathroom.* She goes back to the bathroom and pulls the box of lozenges out of her jean pocket, leaving the jeans on the bathroom floor. *I'll get those later.* She throws the lozenges on the bed and gets her two secret admirer notes out of her drawer, laying them on the bed too. She grabs her cellular phone, slips under the covers, and texts Cecilia:

> guess wat
> Cecilia: ummm, idk?
> Violet forwards the first message from S.A. to her friend.
> Cecilia: omg!!! wen did u get that?!!
> Violet: awile ago. theres more
> Cecilia: from who???
> Violet: idk. today he left cough drops in my jacket :)))
> Cecilia: yay!!! i want 1
> Cecilia: secret admirer, not cough drop (yuk)
> Violet: hehe. weird tho, rite?
> Cecilia: wat do other texts say?
> Violet: hang on

She flattens the notes on her bed, clicks pictures of them and of the box of lozenges, then sends it all to Cecilia.

> Cecilia: that is sooooo cool
> Violet: ik, rite? but idk, kinda stalkerish
> Cecilia: yeah, we gota find out who it is. did u tell tonya? desmond?
> Violet: no and no. i don't wanna tell D mite piss him off
> Cecilia: true

The girls text back and forth for over an hour. Cecilia suggests some names, but there is no good reason to think it's one person over any other. They agree to keep Tonya out of it and begin fishing for clues on Monday. If they drop hints in front of other people, they should be able to figure it out. Creepy stalker dude, or hopeless romantic... time will tell.

16

Violet, Cecilia, and Tonya all have first period together, so they avoid talking about S.A. until third period, when it's just Violet and Cecilia. The mystery of the secret admirer has taken on a whole new meaning since Violet let in a conspirator. *Who is the secret admirer???* The question looms, adding an undertone of adventure to an already exciting week. *Grease!*

Violet slides into the desk next to Cecilia. Cecilia's a good influence because she always sits near the front of the class, and Violet has to admit she listens better when she sits up here. Left to herself, she will sit in the back row every time. She leans over with a scheming grin and makes a show of darting her eyes back and forth across the classroom, then in a stage whisper, "so what's the plan?"

"Idiot," Cecilia laughs. She looks around nonchalantly. "Okay, I'm gonna make a script for after class, when the bell rings. We can start now if I get it done quick enough." Cecilia tears a sheet of paper out of her spiral and starts writing. Violet looks over her shoulder. "Shoo! I need to concentrate."

"Fine," Violet feigns offense. "I'll write my own script. See whose is better." The girls jot notes on their 'scripts' throughout class. *Life is good. I'm glad I have a secret admirer. Maybe it's John Hampton... that would be nice. Hehe!* John is a junior, quarterback on the varsity football team, a guitar player, and a pretty awesome songwriter. He is also hot as all get out. *But he's not in the play... who is in the play? Oh, God, I hope it's not Fynn... gross.* Fynn is a sophomore who has made no secret of his crush on Violet. He is well liked among his peers, but Violet and her friends find him cocky and unattractive, with his skinny arms and hair that always sticks up. *No way... he's not slick enough. He would be bragging to all his little friends. Must be John!*, she kids herself happily.

The bell will ring in five minutes. Cecilia passes her script to Violet. It reads:

> C: So Vi, how's your throat? (Violet got her voice back on Saturday, but she was congested really bad all day. Sunday she was getting better, and this morning her throat was fine. She just has the littlest bit of congestion in her nose.)
> V: Better. I took some cough drops that really helped (we need to look around at this part and see who's paying attention)

Mmmmm... smart girl. Violet smiles and nods as she reads.

> C: Oh good. Cough drops are really good for a sore throat. I'm glad you thought of that.
> V: Yeah, I'm glad someone thought of it.

Violet chuckles and writes at the bottom of the page: *you are stupid* ☺. She turns the page sideways to show it to Cecilia, which earns her a smile and a wink. Violet adds, *you look left and I'll look right.* Cecilia nods, and the bell rings.

The plan doesn't go as smoothly as they hoped. First off, there is confusion as to which left is left, and whose right is where. Once they figure that out, half the class is already filing out of the room, and Violet has missed her next cue. She can't remember what she was supposed to say anyway, so she improvises with a curiously loud, "I LOVE COUGH DROPS!"

The girls burst into laughter, too embarrassed to look around for suspicious reactions. Not that it would have helped, anyway. The whole class is either intentionally ignoring them or staring at them quizzically. "Wow," Cecilia shakes her head, grinning widely, "what a total fail."

■ ■ ■

The rest of the week flies by like a whirlwind. There are shows Thursday, Friday, and Saturday night. Mom and Dad were both supposed to come Thursday, but Dad never made it. He sent her a text to say good luck, and that was it. *It was probably Donna's idea to send the text. In fact, it was probably Donna who sent it. Maybe he'll make it tonight or Saturday.* Mom was kind enough to point out the wrong turn Violet made during 'You're the One That I Want' on the ride home last night, and had some great suggestions for how to get it right tonight. *Thanks Mom, cause you're such an expert dancer. I thought I did pretty good!* Mom must have seen the look on Violet's face, cause she followed it up with a compliment on Violet's solo, but Violet had heard all she needed to hear. *She can't help it. I'm not Maggie. It's not her fault she thinks I'm awful and Maggie is her queen. Good for them. At least they make each other happy.*

Tonight's show should be fun. Maggie and Michael are coming. They'll be taking Violet home. And Desmond's parents are coming too. *They're so cool.* Desmond will come tomorrow so they can hang out afterward. Violet's not going out tonight. She's still not totally over her cold, and she wants to be rested for the show. So far so good, but she's not gonna push it. And it'll be fun hanging out with Maggie and Michael. *Maggie's really chilled out since she started dating him.*

Thursday evening, there was an envelope with her name on it propped against the dressing room mirror. She knew right away who it was from, so she made sure no one was looking when she opened it. She told everyone it was from her mom. Today, she sits on her bed looking at her treasures. She just got home from school, and she has a couple of hours before she needs to be back there. She saved the cough drop box, even though she didn't eat any more of them. *Not a big cough drop fan.* Yesterday's envelope contained a store bought card with a picture of a ballet dancer on the front. Inside, there's a sketch of the dancer all twisted looking, with a surprised expression on her face, and the printing says: Break a Leg! S.A. wrote:

> *Just kidding. You'll be awesome tonight. I told you your throat would get better. Can't wait to see you.*
> *-S.A. :)*
> *P.S. I hope these notes don't freak you out. I promise I'm not a stalker. I just like you and I'm having fun letting you know. Thinking about doing all my relationships like this! LMFAO*

You know, I think I like this guy. I wonder if it's some really ugly kid that I would never even look at normally. She thinks about her friends that are not conventionally attractive. Jamal is really overweight, and Tim has a bad acne problem. *I wish I could write back. If I left a note somewhere for "S.A.", would he get it? He'd have to. Where could I leave it?*

Things between Violet and Desmond have been different lately. Ever since the fight between Violet and Mom, there has been a distance between them. She doesn't really tell him about her problems, and he doesn't ask. *I think he likes it this way.* Violet kind of feels like the only way to keep him interested is to pretend that everything's okay. *And most of the time it is! But when Dad doesn't show up for a play, or Mom can't find anything good to say about my performance, that hurts, and I want to be able to tell him about it. Shoot, I want him to know that hurts without me having to tell him.*

Violet still lets Desmond know when *he* does something she's not happy with. Last weekend, he was supposed to pick her and Tonya up so they could watch his soccer game. His coach had them scrimmaging with another team or something. It's not like Violet even wanted to go watch the game; she was sick and it was cold and nasty out. She was going to support him. But he called up fifteen minutes after he was supposed to get her and said that he was running behind and had to go straight to the game.

She had just been arguing with Tonya about what a good boyfriend he is. Tonya thinks he's boring, and was complaining that he always wants

Violet to follow his schedule, but he never does the things that she wants him to do. And right in the middle of Violet saying how caring and attentive he is, he calls up with that bullcrap. It was embarrassing, it hurt, and she told him so: "so I'm sitting here waiting for you, and you just call me up out of the blue and tell me you don't have time for me?!"

He acted like it was no big deal, "Vi, I didn't say I don't have time for you. I'm behind and I need to get to the game. I'll come by afterwards."

Just like Tonya said. "Well, afterwards may be too late. I have other things to do besides just sit around waiting for you."

"Okay." He sounded as cool as a cucumber. "I'll call you tomorrow, okay?"

Asshole. "Whatever." And she hung up.

She texted him that night at about 10:00, and he didn't respond. *Jerk.* The next day he explained that he had been tired and went to bed early. She didn't buy it, but she let it go anyway. *Whatever. You were probably out with your friends, talking to some other girl. I don't care. I don't need you, anyway.* Yes, things have definitely changed between them.

The show on Friday night feels a lot smoother than Thursday did, and the last show on Saturday is a screaming success. Violet feels on top of the world at curtain call, and for the first time in their relationship, she finds herself really wishing Desmond wasn't around. Heather invited the whole cast back to her house after the show. She still can't stand Heather, but it would be nice to hang out with the cast one last time before Grease becomes total old news. She goes home with Desmond because she told him she would, but she can't help feeling a little deflated as she watches her castmates take off together, pumped for a night of revelry, while she's stuck catering to Desmond's boring self.

WINTER

17

It has been a mild winter so far. There was snow in mid December, a few days after Violet's play, but nothing for Christmas. *Thank God.* Rachel has a light week planned. She's out of school for winter break, and the week between Christmas and New Year's is always slow at work. January will be another story. She left work at 2:00 today and went straight to the gym, which is where she is now, freshening up after a good workout. She did an extra 20 minutes on the elliptical machine in honor of the holidays. *Eat more, exercise more.*

Rachel was surprised when Matt called last week to wish her a Merry Christmas. He called her at work the day before Christmas Eve. He's got her cell phone number, but it would have been awkward for him to call her at home so close to the holidays, a little too familiar. *He's a nice guy. He has good sense.* They had become chummy at school, but Rachel didn't think she'd hear from him over break. It was her idea to meet him for a cup of coffee. *I haven't made new friends in years. It's like a breath of fresh air to talk to somebody whose life is so different from mine. Why shouldn't we be friends?*

Unlike Rachel, Matt works in the accounting department of a large corporation. He'll be extra busy at work this week, what with so many of his co-workers on vacation. She chose a coffee shop near his office so it would be easy for him to meet her. Rachel knows all the coffee shops in and around Franklin, being a bit of a coffee junky. This European style café and bakery is busy during the week, but most people get their coffee to go, so there will be plenty of open tables. She takes her time driving into the city. Traffic is light, and she's feeling relaxed at the end of a hectic month.

There are about 8 people in line at the café when Rachel walks in, and Matt doesn't seem to be here yet. The soothing aroma of rich, fresh coffee welcomes her. *Should I sit up front so he can see me easily, or toward the back where it's quieter?* She pauses a moment, perusing her surroundings. *I want to be able to hear myself think.* She marches past the line to the tables near the back wall and sits at a two top facing the door. She positions her purse on the floor at her feet and unbuttons her coat, but doesn't remove it. She reaches into her coat pocket, pulls out her Blackberry, and places it on the table in front of her. The scent of sugary pastry hangs in the air, mixing with the coffee to create a bouquet of coziness. The sudden recollection of a neighborhood donut shop she lived near as a child puckers her brow. She used to walk past it with her younger brothers, and the owner would occasionally run outside with hot donuts for the boys. It perturbed her that they accepted the gifts so freely, yet a part of her longed to experience that same sense of freedom, that blissful ignorance of consequence, of strings attached.

Matt's voice breaks her reverie. "Rachel, hi! Merry Christmas!" He leans down to kiss her cheek, as if they were old friends.

He is sitting opposite her before she has registered his greeting, simultaneously taking off his coat and draping it backwards over the chair. *He's beautiful. What?!!* Her own thought catches her by surprise. *For a young man.* That's better. "Hi. Merry Christmas to you," she smiles at him. "How *was* your Christmas?"

"Oh, fabulous. There is nothing better than seeing those kids' faces on Christmas morning. *Man*, I love that." He is immediately at home in the café chair, as if he were sitting in his own kitchen. No getting his bearings, no fidgeting or adjusting.

A waitress comes over from behind the bar and takes their order. Rachel orders a latte with a sprinkle of nutmeg. She doesn't need to specify what size, what kind of milk, or how much foam she wants. The drink will come in a standard size mug, and it will taste just how it's supposed to taste... delicious. Matt orders a black coffee and an éclair.

"You know, I am so glad we've had the opportunity to work together," Matt shares as they sip their drinks. "I really admire you."

"You do?"

"I do," he looks at her thoughtfully. "Are you surprised by that?"

"Well, I'm not sure what there is to admire? Do you mean my business? Anyone can do that."

"The business is part of it... a big part of it. But it's not just that. It's the whole picture. Successful business, raising two teenagers alone, going back to grad school. That's serious stuff. Not to mention, you're quite brilliant. I don't know if you realize that."

"Hmph. If I were brilliant, would I be stuck raising two teenagers by myself?" *Whoops. I'm not sure I should have gone there with him.* Rachel looks into her mug of coffee as she takes a sip. *Sorry, Matt. Feel free to change the subject.*

Matt is undaunted. "Even brilliant people can have problems in their relationships. Not that I consider myself brilliant, but I'm not in my first marriage either." He waits for Rachel's response.

He's on his second wife? "How old are you?!!" *Geez, Rachel, you're making yourself look like an old geezer. He's not that young.*

"Thirty-eight. I married Renee when I was thirty, but I was twenty-four when I got married the first time."

"Really?" *Now this is interesting.* "No kids?"

"Nope. I dated Maria for a year. We thought we were in love, got engaged, got married in Aruba. Little wedding with close friends and family. We were together for two years after that. It just wasn't meant to be."

"Huh." *Very interesting.*

"See, you've never let your personal life get in the way of your career. When my first marriage went to hell, I was a wreck. I didn't even work for awhile, and when I did, I wasn't using my CPA. I worked in a damned distribution center, loading boxes, for Christ's sake. It was stupid. I was stupid. But you're brilliant. I was so happy when we got grouped together for the final project. You're a machine!"

Rachel is flattered. "Well, thank you. And I don't think you're stupid at all. You were young, and you were hurt. I'm sure you've grown up since then." *Not to mention, if you were a mom, you wouldn't have had time to fall to pieces.*

"Well, hopefully I won't have to find out," he grins.

Rachel and Matt chat easily. He talks about his kids, she talks about hers. They talk about career goals, personal goals, and where they see themselves in twenty years. They have been chatting for over an hour when she looks at her watch. "Wow, it's almost 5:30. I'm sure you've got to get back to the office. I'm so glad we got together today."

"Yeah, this was nice," he replies. "We'll have to do it again sometime. It's nice to talk to somebody that's not looking for me to turn in paper-work or meet a deadline or mow the lawn," he says with a chuckle. "I do have to close out a couple of things at the office, though."

Rachel picks her purse up off the floor and stands to say goodbye. "It's good to see you, Matt." She drops her Blackberry into her pocket. "We'll talk soon."

Matt stands and leans in to kiss her cheek, putting one hand on her arm. "Happy New Year, Rachel. Have a good evening."

She backs away, smiling at him. "You too!" And heads out to her car.

Rachel feels content driving home tonight. Matt is right; she should be proud of herself. Maggie is about to graduate with honors, she has performed well enough to get into any college she chooses, and she has decided to stay close to home. Violet's a little more iffy, but she did a sensational job in the school musical. *I hope she gets a lead next year. That would be so good for her.* The house will be paid for in five years, Rachel's car is already paid for, and the girls' college funds are in decent shape.

Things at home have been going relatively smoothly, which isn't always the case this time of year. When Rachel and Violet had that big blow-out right before Thanksgiving, Rachel had thought that all her fears about Violet were about to come true: drugs, sex, teen pregnancy. *Thank heavens for small blessings.* Violet has actually been doing really well. Her room is still a danger zone, and the girls still argue about keeping the bathroom clean, but at least her mess is somewhat contained. There was a time when Violet could wreck the entire house just from being in it for a couple of hours. Violet's spending less time with her Dad, which is a good thing. *She is always so irritable and emotional when she's been around him. It's amazing he hasn't disappeared altogether by now.* The girls were pleased with their Christmas gifts... *clothes and money, easy peasy.* In fact, the only clothes Rachel bought were things the girls had picked out themselves. She did get Maggie that writing set, though. *She seemed to really enjoy that.*

Violet's spending New Year's weekend with Cecilia. They are going to visit Cecilia's family in the mountains... *a cousin or aunt or something?* Rachel is just glad she won't have to worry about keeping tabs on her. She's even going to a party this New Year's Eve. *I have to figure out what I'm going to wear.* Maggie has a party to go to with Michael, but that's nothing to worry about. Maggie won't cause any trouble. Rachel goes back to the conversation she had with Matt about goals, plans, and where they'll be in twenty years. She enjoys thinking about the future, about life without children at home. She imagines meeting an adult Maggie out for a drink, chatting about life, men, opportunities. It's harder to picture what her relationship with an adult Violet will be like. *She'll probably want to have as little to do with me as possible. Oh well, as long as I've done my job as a mother, I'm not going to worry about what she thinks of me. She'll get it someday.* Rachel sinks into the cushiony back of the driver's seat, and for a moment, all is right with the world.

18

"Violet, let's go!" Cecilia calls through the house.

Aaaah, I'm coming, I'm coming. "Be right there!" Violet calls back. She grabs her coat and boots and runs down the stairs. They are actually staying at Cecilia's mother's cousin's house. It's a beautiful place just outside of a small mountain town. Violet is struck by the quaintness of it. She has no idea how expensive a place like this is, ten minutes outside of downtown in a popular tourist area. The yard is thick with snow covered pine trees, the ground is buried three feet deep in places, and the shoveled front walk is frosted with this morning's flurries.

Cecilia stands by the front door waiting for Violet, and examines her humorously when she screeches to a stop in front of her. "What are you going to do with those?" she asks, indicating the boots.

"Huh? I'm wearin em," Violet explains, waiting for Cecilia to open the door so they can hurry to the car.

"You do know there's snow on the ground," Cecilia hints.

It takes a minute, then "Ooooh, good point." Violet sits on the stairs to don her boots and coat, then hops up. "Ok, let's go!"

Cecilia's mother, aunt (for all intents and purposes), and two younger 'cousins' are waiting in the car to head to the ski slopes. The cousins are 12-year-old Fernando and 10-year-old Jessica. Unlike Cecilia and her older brother, who were born in Venezuela and raised by their grandmother until Cecilia was seven, Fernando and Jessica were both born in the United States. Violet doesn't really get the relationship between Cecilia's mother and her aunt. Her mother is a quiet, shy, working class type with almost no English, whereas her aunt is a perfectly polished, educated, white collar professional with perfect English. Yet when they are together, they act like best friends.

Cecilia's aunt, known as Tia, drives a big, black, four-wheel-drive SUV with three rows of seats. Fernando and Jessica are seated in the way back, leaving plenty of room for Violet and Cecilia to stretch out in the middle row. Violet has been skiing a few times before, but she's not very good at it. She hopes Cecilia isn't too much of an expert. "Does your mom ski?"

"Pfffft," Cecilia smirks. "Can you picture my mom skiing?"

"Yeah, not so much, I guess. What else is there to do there?"

"Oh, you know, the usual. There's a café and an arcade in the lodge. They've got a big stone fireplace. It's awesome when it snows at night. Too bad Cam and Desmond couldn't be here."

"Yeah, I know," Violet agrees blandly. She is checking out the amazing views from the car window as the road twists up the side of the mountain. Where it is hemmed in on both sides by trees, it feels like Mother Nature has crafted a kaleidoscope out of branches and tree trunks and pine needles, and they are driving through it. In a lot of spots, it is sheer cliff on one side of the road, and an open view of the adjacent mountains on the other. Violet tries to see into the woods below them, imagining all the life that hides within. In the distance, the wooded mountains are an impenetrable network of dips and swells, drawing her in even as they shut her out. You can look, but you can't touch. It's mesmerizing. *Oh, yeah, Cecilia.* Violet turns toward her friend. "What's Cam doing for New Year's?"

"He's going to Evan's."

"Oh, right. How was that last year?" Last New Year's Eve, Violet had found herself totally smashed, hanging out with Tonya at some 20-year-old guy's house with a bunch of his reject high school dropout friends. It was not pretty.

Violet tried alcohol for the first time her freshman year of high school, hanging out with Tonya, Teah, Jamal, and Chris after the Freshman Fall Fling. Actually, they started drinking at the Fall Fling, and then just kept going. That summer, she added weed and pills to her repertoire, and had sex for the first time, three times actually, with some creeper that she would prefer not to remember. It was a bad summer. In retrospect, it was a bad year, from the first time she tried alcohol. It occurs to her as she chats amicably with Cecilia, not two feet from Cecilia's mother, that last New Year's was the last time she got really drunk. She had only been dating Desmond a few weeks at the time, and he was away with his family for the holidays. He got really mad at her when he found out about her escapade. She used that as her excuse to stop doing that kind of shit. Truthfully, she was glad to have an excuse. It was embarrassing, and usually not that fun anyway.

"It was fun," Cecilia answers, not noticing any change in Violet's train of thought. "What's Des doing tomorrow?"

"I don't know. He hadn't decided the last time I talked to him. He'll probably know when I call him tonight. We're just staying at the house, right?"

"Yeah. Is that cool with you?"

"Yeah, that's fine. I like your family."

"Thanks, girlie. I like your family too. Next year, though, we're gonna have to tear the roof off somewhere."

"Agreed."

"What do you mean *next* year?" Tia interjects from the driver's seat. "Waddya think we're going to be doing tomorrow, chicas? I'm ready to party! Jessica, you have your sequined dress ready?"

"Yup! And the party hats too!"

"All right! Fernando, you got your dancing shoes shined?"

"Yeah, Ma," he replies sarcastically.

"What?" Cecilia teases, "you're not gonna salsa with me, Fernando?"

"I don't think so." His tone remains sarcastic, but he is holding back a smile.

"You ever see Yolanda salsa?" Tia asks Violet, referring to Cecilia's mother.

"Uh uh," Violet responds.

"Oooh, this woman can move. Fernando, you need to dance with the girls, cause your Papi can't handle all of us."

"That's true." Fernando takes the bait and ups the ante. "But I don't want Papi to feel bad, cause I *can* handle you all. No one's gonna wanna dance with Papi anymore after they see *me* salsa."

Cecilia's mom laughs and turns to look at him, throwing a wink at Violet as she speaks. "¡Escucha ese hombrecito, ya se pensando mejor que el padre!" And as she turns back, "vamos ver quien puede bailar."

"You hear that, Nandito?" Tia asks her son. "Your tia's gonna put you to the test. You can't just tell her you're better than your Papi. You're gonna have to prove it."

Cecilia's mom says something to Tia in Spanish, and the kids are no longer in their conversation. Jessica, sitting behind Cecilia on the passenger side, leans forward and taps Violet on the shoulder. "Do you know how to dance salsa?"

She's so cute. "No, but I like to dance."

"Good! We'll teach you how, right Nando?"

"Sure." Now that the joking is over, he's slipped back into 'I'm a cool teenager' mode. Not rude, just sort of detached and aloof. He pulls out a handheld gaming device and forgets about the others.

"Cecilia said you were the star of the school musical," Jessica says enthusiastically.

"No, not the star." Violet demurs. "Do you know the movie Grease?"

"No."

"Cecilia," Violet scolds, "she's never seen Grease?"

"Don't look at me," Cecilia protests. "We need to get you that movie, Jess. We were ten when we started watching it, weren't we?" she asks Violet.

"That's right! We were so into it. Jessica, you have got to see it. It rocks. I was one of the Pink Ladies."

"Cool!" 'Pink Lady' means nothing to Jessica, but she clearly looks up to the older girls, so anything they do must be cool.

■ ■ ■

It is a long, fun day on the ski slopes. Tia is apparently an excellent skier, but she doesn't ski today, opting to hang out with Yolanda instead. Cecilia, Jessica, and Fernando are all really good too. Cecilia only does a couple of runs with her cousins, spending most of the day with Violet on the beginner slopes instead. The resort is crowded, making it feel like a party all day long. It's now 7:30 in the evening. Violet and Cecilia are curled up in armchairs in the lodge sipping hot cocoa. The flagstone fireplace is enormous, and they can feel its toasty warmth even from halfway across the room. They have been in and out of the lodge all day, but this is the first time they've taken off all their layers and been still long enough to appreciate how cozy it is.

"How long til fireworks?" Violet asks Cecilia.

"They start at 8:00. I think we can see them from here. Do you wanna go outside in case we can't?"

"Nah. I'm too comfortable. We've seen fireworks before. Do you?"

"I'm with you. I'm done being cold for the day."

Good. "Have you ever been here for New Year's Eve?"

"No. They do a pretty nice show the night before, though. Tia says New Year's Eve here is crazy. We should come back sometime and check it out, just the two of us."

"That would be the shit."

"Yeah, she said we could come up anytime. Did you ever find out what Des is doing tomorrow?"

"No," Violet pulls her cell phone out of her back pocket. "I'm gonna ask him." She only looks at her phone for a second to type before turning back to Cecilia, cell phone at the ready for a response to the 'hey boo' she texted Desmond. "Your aunt rocks," Violet comments. "I'm kinda glad we're not going out tomorrow night."

"Me too. We can drink with my aunt, too. I mean, not get drunk, but she'll have champagne and stuff."

"Nice. And I wouldn't get drunk in front of your family." *She knows that, right?*

"I know, girl. I wonder what Cam's doing..." Cecilia pulls out her phone and types a message.

Violet looks at her phone. Nothing yet. *Where's my boo?* She types again: hello? A minute later, her phone buzzes in her hand:

eatin dinner. hold up

She texts him back, 'k.' *I miss my man.* Cecilia is busy texting back and forth with Cam. Violet looks around at the mix of people in the lodge. Young, old, and in between. Families, couples, singles. There's a group of hot guys walking through the lobby, laughing and talking. *I don't want you, I want my boo,* she thinks. She looks at her phone again, willing it to vibrate, then types: i miss you. Nothing. She gives up and texts Tonya instead: hey!

This time, the response is almost instant: hey you! wassup?

Violet: chilin in ski lodg. u?

Tonya: bitch

Violet: don't hate

Tonya: ha! gues wat?!

Violet: ?

Tonya: goin to party with D tomoro

What? Why would Desmond take Tonya to a party? She types back: uh, ok?

Tonya: hehe. ikr? ran in2 him and J at cofee shop. he misses u

Violet: he better! so? *At least he apparently doesn't hate Tonya anymore.* He has been less skeptical of her since they talked about her at that party on Thanksgiving. Less critical. And she has kind of chilled out lately.

Tonya: st. ant party. i'm goin with them

Violet: cool

Violet's phone rings. It's Desmond. *Bye Tonya*. She answers the call. "Hey Babe!"

"Hey! I miss you too."

"Why, thank you. Watcha doin?"

"Just ate. How bout you?"

"Sitting in a ski resort, by a big fire, drinking hot chocolate and thinking about you."

"Wow, I wish I could be there with you."

"Me too." *I really do.* Violet has felt less close to Desmond lately, but all of a sudden, being so far away, she realizes how much he means to her. Maybe he's not perfect, maybe he can't fill her up completely, but he's still a huge part of her life. "I hear you're going to a party with Tonya tomorrow?"

"Yeah. You talk to her?"

"She just texted me. You and Jaden are going?"

"Yeah. It's this kid that graduated St. Anthony's last year. He's been having parties for a couple of years. I didn't know if he was gonna throw one this year, but he is. Jaden invited Tonya, but I'm cool with it. She's pretty chill."

"Well I'm glad you guys are hanging out together. You know, I think she may actually be growing up a little." Violet thought Tonya was full of crap when she said she was turning over a new leaf after Marcus, but she really has been different since then.

Violet and Desmond chat for about twenty minutes. They talk about New Year's plans, they talk about school. Desmond has submitted all his college applications, and Violet realizes that she hasn't made as big a deal about it at she probably should have. She's been so caught up in her own life that she hasn't paid a lot of attention to his. *I need to do something special for him, to celebrate.* It is starting to get loud in the lodge, so Violet says goodbye, promising to text him again before she goes to bed.

19

It turns out the girls *are* able to see the fireworks from their seats in the lodge. Afterwards, they meet Cecilia's family at the snack counter, as previously arranged, and head back to the house to settle in for the night. Once showered and in their pajamas, Violet and Cecilia make themselves another round of hot cocoa and carry it into the den, where they have been sleeping on a foldout couch. It's a smallish room, but everything in it looks like it was made for the space. A big comfy couch (the one they are sleeping on), and a straight back brown leather armchair, a built-in entertainment center in dark wood, with a flat screen television on one end and a desktop computer on the other. The walls are a warm green, and it has hardwood floors with a big oriental rug in muted browns and burgundies and greens. On the wall adjacent to the entertainment center, children's artwork hangs in large frames. One is a collage in bright colors, another is a painting of a tree and the moon. *The kids must have done those forever ago.* And yet somehow they add to the sophistication of the space.

Violet sets her hot chocolate gently down on a side table and crawls into bed, pulling the covers up over her legs. She scoots back so that she is cradled in the corner of the couch and pulls her knees up toward her chin. "Today was so much fun!"

Cecilia grabs a throw off the arm of the couch and sits in the armchair, curling her legs up under her. "I know. I'm so glad you came." She has put her mug on the table next to her. She drapes the throw over her legs and tucks it under her feet. "So what did you and Des talk about tonight?" Cecilia sounds serious, picking up on Violet's thoughtful mood.

"Nothing really." Violet reaches for her hot chocolate. "Oh, Tonya's going to a New Year's Eve party with Desmond and Jaden." Saying it out loud, she notices a slight pang of jealousy somewhere in her chest, just above her stomach. Or maybe it's in her stomach, but it's definitely jealousy.

"Yeah, I heard you saying something about that. I thought he hated her?"

"I guess he's okay with her now. She really hasn't done anything stupid in awhile. Anyway, I think Jaden invited her." *Okay, that's better. I have nothing to be jealous of. He's just taking her to be nice.*

"Jaden's cool. I like him. Do you think he's into Tonya?"

"Isn't everybody? It's bright in here." Violet pushes the covers down off her legs and turns the lamp on next to the couch.

Cecilia tracks her with her eyes as she walks to the door to turn off the overhead light, and remarks, "you're right about Tonya changing, but Tonya will always be Tonya. I haven't always felt like you were you."

Violet has just flicked off the light. She turns around to look at Cecilia, surprised. "You haven't?"

The girls are still, each examining the other. "Uh uh. When we were in elementary and middle school, you were always the responsible one. You just kind of stayed in the background, only poking your head out when you had to defend somebody else. Don't you remember how shy and quiet you were?"

I was, wasn't I? She climbs back into bed, sitting upright this time, crosslegged. "Yeah, I guess I was..." Violet is apprehensive. *So if I was responsible then, what am I now?*

"You're not like that at all anymore, and you kind of changed all of a sudden. In high school. Like you went from being totally timid and scared, to being this wild, crazy... I don't know. You kinda went crazy for awhile there."

Ooookay. I don't really know what to say to that. She laughs awkwardly, "yeah, I guess I did."

"I'm glad you're not so wild and crazy anymore. For awhile there, I was afraid I had lost you."

Huh?!! "Whaddyu mean? You never lost me!"

"I know. I just couldn't hang with you for awhile. It seemed like you were always on something, and, no offense, but always hanging out with messed up people."

"Huh." Violet holds her hot chocolate in her lap and plays over its surface with her index finger. *Wow. We didn't hang out as much last year, but I thought we were still friends. That's messed up.*

"Violet, I'm not trying to piss you off. I just missed you then. You're not yourself when you're drunk or high. Nobody is. I mean, you never did anything to me. I wasn't mad at you. It hurt."

Fuck... she's right, isn't she? Damn. I was like my fucking Dad. As much as Violet doesn't like to admit it, even to herself, her Dad has hurt her a lot. Over and over and over again. She meets Cecilia's eyes. "I'm sorry, C. I don't mean to be like that."

Cecilia smiles at her. She walks over and climbs across the mattress, giving her friend a kiss on the cheek, then plopping down next to her. "You're *not* like that. Tonya's always gonna be wrapped up in guys and partying and bullshit. That's just Tonya. That's what I like about Tonya. But that's not you and that's not me. I'm a nerd, and you're a performer. That's who we are, and we're awesome at it."

The mood shifts in the room, brightening like a match to a candle. "You're not a nerd, dumbass. You're a genius! A freaking mastermind! The next Nobel Laureate!"

"Hah! And you're the next... really famous, but really good singer!"

"The next Barbara Streissand!"

"Oh God," Cecilia shakes her head vigorously. "I HATE Barbara Streissand!"

Violet laughs. "I know. I hate her too, but she is really famous and she can really sing!"

Cecilia raises her fist. "The next Barbara Streissand!"

Violet raises both fists. "The next Einstein!" They laugh loudly for a moment, then both seem to realize it's too late to be making such a ruckus.

Violet lies down on her side, one arm bent to hold her head up, facing Cecilia. "So, I've made a decision."

Cecilia lies facing Violet in the same position, back a little bit so they're not in each other's faces. "Uh huh?"

"You know things have been kinda dead between Desmond and me lately?"

"No, but okay?"

"I don't know. I just haven't been opening up to him. Ever since my mom hit me that time, I've had a different attitude toward him. He really pissed me off the way he handled that. But I realized, we had a great relationship before that. And the only thing that changed was me. He still treats me well. I mean, he's not perfect, but he's good."

"I agree."

"So why should I let one stupid night ruin everything for us? I mean, like I said, he's not perfect. Neither am I! He's gonna be going off to college in a few months, and I don't want to lose him. He's too good of a guy for that."

"Good for you. And you're right. Like Cam can be a total airhead, but that's just Cam! I can take it personally when he forgets things or makes us late or something, but for what? He always feels bad about it, he tries to be better, and he is so great in other ways. He'll do anything for anybody, he's a total romantic. He always sends me little surprise notes or buys me little presents… speaking of which, whatever happened to your secret admirer?" The girls never did much to find out his identity, what with the musical and finals and Christmas. That first week, they did a couple more "skits" to try and lure him out, but with no luck.

"Hmph! So much for 'patiently waiting'! Nothing since the break-a-leg card. Worthless! Men are all the same!" Violet jokes.

"No doubt! Do you still have the notes?"

"Of course! I'm saving those, so I can show my kids how awesome I was."

"Nice. But I don't think you're gonna have to prove that to them. Or, actually, they probably won't believe you if you try. You ever met a kid that thought their mom was awesome as a teenager?"

"Not so much," agrees Violet. "So I guess I need to keep them to remind *me* how awesome I was."

"Yup! Almost as awesome as me." Cecilia teases. The girls chat a little longer before falling into a sleepy, companionable silence.

20

New Year's Eve is fun with Cecilia's family. They all stay up until 2:00 in the morning, even Jessica and Fernando. Violet speaks to Desmond on the phone at about 12:15, but he's at a party and it's loud, so they just talk for a minute. When she wakes up late on Sunday, New Year's Day, she has a text from him. He sent it at 7am. *Wow, he was up early.* It says: miss you, sexy. can't wait to see you monday. *Aaaawww.* She smiles widely. *That's my baby.* She types back: hey babe. can't wait 2 c u too!!! i luv u. At home, Mom always plans a big New Year's Day dinner, but Cecilia's family did their big dinner late on New Year's Eve, so Violet's last day in the mountains is a quiet one.

Violet gets home midday on Monday; school starts back Tuesday. She has been texting Desmond all day. In fact, he texted her all day yesterday *and* today. *It feels like when we first started dating. I love him!!!* They have already planned for him to come by and get her this afternoon. She just has to clean her room before she goes out. Violet didn't know what Mom was talking about on the phone when she called her and said she had to clean today, but when she walks into her bedroom, she realizes the empty clothing boxes stacked in the corner and the new clothes scattered about the room do look kind of messy. *It's all clean, though, and at least the boxes are in the corner. It's not like I just left them everywhere. I don't know why she even cares what my room looks like. It's not like she hangs out in here. It's not like she even comes in here except to find something for me to do. Ughh.*

She drops her overnight bag on her bed and sends Desmond a text: i'm home! need 15 mins 2 clean room. She sticks her phone in her back pocket and gets to work. She finds a gift bag in her closet, and uses it to collect tissue paper from the clothing boxes. There's green and red and silver, and one with a print of the night sky in deep blues and purples… *so pretty.* The gift bag goes in the corner of the closet. She piles up the gift boxes and stacks them on the bag. *Might need those.* As to the clothing, it's hard to put it away when she hasn't yet discovered all the possible combinations she can create. How will she even remember what she has if it's all stuffed in her closet? *Hmmm. Oh well. I should hang it, but I wanna see Desmond! I'll hang it later.* She layers the clothes on top of each other on the bed and opens her dresser drawer: *full. Damn.* She opens another drawer and commences to combine the two, pushing and tucking until the drawer almost closes. *Yay!* She then lays her new clothes in the now empty drawer. She turns around to survey the room, and realizes she still has a pile of lotions, lip balms, costume jewelry, and other Christmas stocking stuffers on her desk. *Mom won't like that.* The doorbell rings. *Quick!* She grabs the whole pile and heads to the bathroom, where she dumps it unceremoniously into her cabinet drawer.

When Violet opens the front door, Desmond is standing in the sun waiting for her. She jumps forward and wraps her arms around him. They hold each other tight for a moment, neither one aware of the frigid air blowing around them. "Hey hottie," Violet intones with her face just centimeters from his.

"Mmmm," he squeezes her tight and kisses her on the lips. "You're the hottie. Watcha wanna do?"

"I don't care." The persistent pressure of the cold day begins to work its way through their embrace, and Violet steps back into the house. "Come inside for a sec." She shuts the door behind him, and they hug again, kissing each other briefly. "No one's home," she remarks suggestively.

"Oh, really?" Desmond asks, rubbing his hands over her back. "Where's Maggie?"

"No idea," Violet kisses his neck and his earlobe. "Does it matter?" She kisses him again, and he kisses her back.

"I wish it didn't," he whispers, "but yeah," he looks at her seriously, "it kinda does. I don't want your family thinking I'm some kind of perv.'"

"Uggh!" Violet slaps his shoulder playfully and grabs his hand. "You're no fun! Let's go get something to eat." She pulls him toward the kitchen.

The sun shines brightly through the large window over the sink, making the room feel warmer than it is. Desmond takes off his puffy down jacket and hangs it on a chair at the kitchen table. Violet is at the fridge, eyeing its contents dubiously. "I guess my Mom didn't cook yesterday." Violet was expecting hordes of leftovers from a big New Year's Day dinner, but Mom and Maggie actually went to Stephanie's house for their New Year's meal.

Desmond heads to the pantry to check that out. There are several half empty cereal boxes, but nothing good. It's all healthy stuff. There's a small assortment of canned beans, a box of spaghetti and a couple of jars of tomato sauce, a box of Bisquick, a box of Wheat Thins, bags of flour and sugar. Violet stands next to Desmond, feeling equally disappointed. "Where's all your food?" he asks.

"We never have any food," she answers. "Wheat Thins?"

"Sure." Neither one of them is pleased with their find.

Violet grabs the box of crackers and heads back to the fridge. "I think we have some cream cheese," she says, pulling open the door. "And, oooh," she sounds inspired, "orange juice." She grabs the container, immediately disappointed by the hollow sloshing sound within. "Okay, maybe we don't have orange juice. Milk?" she asks her boyfriend, putting the orange juice back on the shelf.

"Eew, just the crackers," Desmond is quick to respond as he sits at the table.

Violet leaves the milk in the fridge and gets out a half empty tub of plain cream cheese. She tucks the box of crackers under her arm and gets a butter knife out of a drawer on her way to the table. "Better than nothing," she declares, laying the snack out between them. She begins spreading cream cheese on crackers, placing them up for grabs on the table. "So how was your New Year's?" she asks between bites.

"Okay," Desmond responds noncommittally. "How was yours?"

"I already told you about mine!" Violet protests. "Tell me about the party. Did Tonya behave?"

"She was fine. It was just a party. You weren't there. Does that answer your question?" Desmond asks, looking at her meaningfully.

Could you be any more awesome? Violet is moved by his comment. She feels a hollow in her chest as she meets his gaze, an opening up. It is a scary, exciting feeling, full of hope. "So in other words, it sucked?" She is joking, but he is not.

"Yes. It sucked. I don't ever want to spend another New Year's Eve without you. I don't ever want to spend another day without you. I love you, Violet. More than anything."

Wow, this is a little intense. He is not smiling at all. His eyes are fixed on her, almost pleading. He seems nervous too. *Why are you so emotional?* Violet needs to cut the tension. "I love you too, crazy," she announces cheerily. "I'm gonna go get my coat." She pushes back from the table and heads up to her room, where she took her coat off earlier. *Okay, that was a little weird. I guess he really missed me!* Violet's grin seems to start in her heart and carry all the way through her body to her lips, and she wears it proudly the whole rest of the day.

21

The first week of the year, everything is fantastic. Since it's a new semester, there's no big projects or tests to worry about. Mom's still on winter break, so she's not all stressed out. She's been taking Maggie to look at cars, so Maggie's happy as a clam. Desmond has basketball at school, but he's still been managing to see Violet every day. She uses her Christmas money to take him out to dinner before his game on Thursday as a celebration of the end of college applications. He's been treating her like gold lately. *I don't know what Tonya was thinking. He doesn't put himself first at all! All I have to do is open up to him, and he's there for me. I don't know why I got so mad at him Thanksgiving week. That was stupid.*

On Friday night, Violet, Desmond, Cecilia, and Cam all go to the movies together, then out to eat burgers. Afterwards, they hang out at Desmond's until late, and Violet hooks up with Desmond again Saturday morning. He picks her up and the two of them spend the afternoon at the mall, where Violet buys a cute t-shirt for Maggie, who has also turned in all her college applications. *She works hard, she deserves it.* The couple is sitting in the Starbucks at the mall when Violet gets a text from Tonya. It's about 3:00. While everyone else seems to be reveling in the joys of the new year, Tonya has been having a hard week. Violet caught her in the bathroom with Teah on Wednesday, and it looked like she had been crying, but she wouldn't tell Violet what was going on. Violet texted her that afternoon, but she said everything was fine. Now, Tonya is inviting her to sleep over tonight. *Shoot. I don't want to, but I know something's going on with her. I need to.* She texts back: sure! wat time? Then addresses Desmond, "I'm going to Tonya's tonight."

He frowns. "I thought we were gonna hang out."

"I know. I would rather hang out with you, but I think something's going on with her. She's been really emotional all week."

Desmond turns to looks out into the mall corridor. He sets his jaw, and Violet sees his neck and shoulders grow tight. "So because she's having a bad week, you need to go be with her." He looks back at Violet. "If you were having a bad week, would she drop her boyfriend to be with you?"

Ummm, drop my boyfriend? "I'm not dropping you, Desmond." *What is wrong with you?* "It's not like we already had plans to hang out. I mean, I know I never said we're *not* hanging out, but we have been hanging out all week. I haven't seen Tonya once."

"Except for going to school with her every day." Desmond glares at her, daring her to disagree.

What the hell? "Oh, please. Like we have so much time to hang out at school. I'm not trying to diss you Desmond. I just need to spend one night with my friend." *Does he need me? Is something going on with him that I don't know about?* "Desmond, I love you. I would much rather hang out with you than Tonya. If you need me, forget about Tonya. I'll be with you. But if you're okay, then I need to go be with my friend. I'll leave early tomorrow and we can hang out again. You can even come pick me up there." She is feeling a little desperate, blindsided. *I don't wanna fight with him. Things have been too good.*

Desmond is sulking now. "Whatever. Go. I'm fine. We'll hang out tomorrow. But I'm not going to pick you up at Tonya's. You can call me when you get home." He is looking out at the mall again, brow creased and lower lip poking out.

Violet is unsure. *Do I cancel on Tonya? What is his deal? Why won't he pick me up at Tonya's? Did she do something he hasn't told me? Whatever. If something happened, Tonya will tell me about it tonight. Maybe she dissed him and Jaden on New*

Year's and hooked up with some loser. I bet that's what happened. She probably hooked up with some creep who screwed her over. That's why she's upset, and Desmond's pissed cause she disappeared. Maybe even dissed Jaden for the creep. "Did something happen with Tonya and Jaden on New Year's?"

Desmond looks surprised, and the jolt seems to distract him from his anger. "No. Not that I know of anyway." He looks thoughtful. "Actually, Jaden cut out early on New Year's. Said he wasn't feeling well." Desmond shrugs, and seems to have forgotten all about being annoyed. "I don't know, maybe they hooked up later or something. I know Jaden thinks she's hot. I told him not to mess with her, though."

"Oh." *Jaden cut out early… so it was just Desmond and Tonya? Huh.* "So who else went with you guys?"

"Huh?" He takes a sip of his coffee, eyebrows raised in question.

"To the party. Did Jaden go with you guys, or what?"

"Yeah, he went. But he was all stuffed up and coughing and his head hurt, so he went home right after midnight. Got a ride with someone from school."

Interesting. You didn't mention that. "So, how late did you and Tonya hang out?" Violet is feeling uncomfortable, but she tries to play it cool. *No reason to get upset.*

"Me and Tonya didn't *hang* out…" he insists.

Is he getting defensive?

"We were at the same party. She hung out with a totally different crowd. Those same guys she met on Thanksgiving. I just took her home."

Oh, okay. Chill out, Violet, she tells herself. *Quit acting like a jealous freak.* "Cool. Thank you for watching out for her."

"Of course," he responds, satisfied. "I told you, Violet, I love you. You never have to worry about me doing anything to hurt you, no matter what anyone else tells you. I want you to know that."

Well, that was an awkward way of phrasing it. No matter what anyone else tells me? Oh, who cares. He told you he loves you and would never hurt you. Quit looking for trouble. "I love you too, Desmond, and I would never hurt you either." They enjoy the next hour together, sipping coffee and watching the passersby, then Desmond takes her home to get ready for her visit with Tonya.

22

The temperature drops sharply Saturday evening. Violet sits at the kitchen table with Mom and Maggie, eating Mom's chicken breasts and rice unenthusiastically. Maggie liked her t-shirt, and is wearing it now under a yellow wool sweater. Violet is wearing baggy gray sweatpants and a black sweatshirt of Desmond's, which is probably what she'll wear to bed tonight at Tonya's. She's also got on her thick, purple, fuzzy socks. She keeps glancing up at the window in anticipation, hoping that the 60% chance of snow will turn out to be 100%. Mom is in a sweatsuit, but her outfit is fitted with a matching green jacket and pants. She's going to drop Violet at Tonya's on the way to the gym.

Mom catches Violet looking toward the window, and follows her gaze. "I hope it doesn't snow," she complains. "Luckily if it does, it should only be flurries."

"I don't know," counters Maggie, "I think I'm ready for a good hard snow. Did it snow while you were in the mountains, Vi?"

"Just a little." *Hurry up and eat so we can go.* "There was snow everywhere, though. It was pretty. I hope it snows too."

"Why do you girls want it to snow? It's not like you'll be out there playing in it." Mom chews every bite thoroughly, taking her time.

"I will!" Violet exclaims. "In fact, I need to bring gloves and extra pants, just in case."

"Oh my God," Maggie laughs. "You are such a dweeb. But don't you think it's pretty, Mom?"

"It's pretty until we need to shovel it, drive in it, scrape it off the car. I'm just fine looking at snow in pictures, thank you. Now if we were out at a ski resort like Violet was, then I'd appreciate the snow." She takes another bite of rice.

What was that, one grain? Eat already! "I'm done." Violet starts to stand up, plate in hand.

"Salad," Mom points with her fork. "In the fridge."

Violet regards her Mom, considering. She's about to clarify that she's not interested in salad, but decides not to make waves. "Kay." She leaves her plate on the table and pulls a glass bowl out of the fridge. "Dressing?"

Mom is cutting her chicken into little pieces. "Just get oil, vinegar, salt, and pepper. Bring it to the table."

"Balsamic," Maggie reminds her.

"Duh," Violet snaps back as she carries everything over. "Cause I usually get... another kind of vinegar."

Mom smirks, but doesn't comment. Violet loads her plate with salad, realizing only after she's done so that she didn't want that much. *Shit.* She glances around the table to see if she's being watched. *Damn.* Four eyes on her. *Guess I gotta eat it.* She dresses her salad and digs in, noticing that Mom and Maggie finally seem to be making progress with their plates.

"So," Maggie breaks the silence, "is it just gonna be you and Tonya tonight?" She uses the side of her fork to scrape leftover tidbits of rice and chicken off to the side of her plate, and serves herself salad.

"I think so," Violet answers around a bite of salad. "I told her to invite Cecilia, but I don't know if she did."

"How *is* Cecilia?" Mom asks. "It doesn't seem like she's been around lately."

"She has, you just haven't seen her. She's good." Violet takes her last bite of salad, and this time she stands up with her plate. "I'm done." She walks to the sink. "I'm going to get my stuff." She rinses her plate and leaves it in the sink, missing the look Mom and Maggie exchange behind her. They're used to getting a minimum of work out of Violet. "Lemme know when you're ready." She heads up to her room.

■ ■ ■

When Violet arrives at Tonya's house, she's relieved to see that Tonya is dressed about like she is, in cotton shorts and an old sweater. There have been plenty of times that Violet thought they were having a girls' night, and it turned out Tonya was all fixed up and they were either going out or having guys over. Tonya's got her hair pulled back in a pony tail and no makeup on, but she looks cheerful enough.

They start out the evening making gooey ooey s'mores in the microwave. Tonya teaches Violet how to melt the chocolate and marshmallows on a buttered plate, then transfer it to the graham crackers with a spatula. It makes for a messy treat, but it sure does taste good! After dessert, they head to Tonya's room to paint their nails. Violet's really good at painting designs, and Tonya has bought two different nail pens especially for the occasion. They find The 40 Funniest Pranks on TV, which makes for good entertainment while they work. When their fingernails are done and they're waiting for them to dry, Violet suggests they find a movie to rent off Netflix. This takes them out of Tonya's room and to the game room, where Violet flops down on one of the two fluffy red couches, figuring Tonya can find the remote quicker than she can. They've brought in supplies to attack their toenails next.

Tonya grabs the remote off the entertainment center and sits on the same couch as Violet. She turns the t.v. on and passes her the remote. "So how was the mountains?" She is facing Violet, with her left ankle tucked under her right thigh.

"Good." Violet gets the movie list up on the screen and props her feet up on the coffee table, leaning back into the couch and turning her head towards Tonya. "How was that New Year's party?" She feels that pressure in the bottom of her chest again. *I know nothing happened to bother me. Still, it will be nice to hear it from her mouth.*

Tonya's face suddenly turns, the corners of her mouth drawing down. She looks down at her lap, where her clasped hands lay. "That's actually what I wanted to talk to you about," she replies.

Violet is silent, waiting. *This better not be about my fucking boyfriend.* But something tells her that it is. Tonya's lips start to quiver, and a tear rolls down her cheek. She is not looking at Violet. *Oh my God, no fucking way. You better tell me this is not about Desmond.* Violet's whole body goes warm, and the pressure in her chest becomes a burning sensation. Her eyes grow moist and her face turns to stone. She remains silent, waiting.

Tonya suddenly pounds her thighs once with clenched fists and lets go a flood of tears. "God, Violet, I'm so sorry! You've known all along, *haven't* you? How could you not say anything?!!" Her face is in her hands now, and she is shaking.

Known all along? What? NO, I didn't know... Should I have known? Violet is thrown off guard.

"Violet, you are so strong. You *know* I was totally hammered, right? I mean, you *know* I would never have done that if I had *known* what I was doing." She is crying freely, and pounds her legs again. "God, I don't even remember what happened! I mean, one minute I'm at a party, knocking back shots, and the next, I wake up in Desmond's bed! I knew I was drinking too much, but I was with *Desmond.* Your *boyfriend.* I never thought he would take advantage of me like that!" Another round of sobs overtakes her.

Violet is surprised to find herself sympathizing with Tonya. *What did he do to her?!!* "Tonya, you really don't remember what happened?" It is hard to get the words out. It feels like someone has their hands around her neck, squeezing steadily. She is still lying back on the couch, her body not yet responding to the tempest in her mind.

Tonya pulls the rubber band out of her hair and fiddles with it between her hands, letting her hair fall forward to cover her face. "I don't remember anything, except waking up with *him.*" She pronounces 'him' as if it were a curse, then looks at Violet. "Vi, I can't tell you how shitty I felt at that moment. I've been in a lot of shitty situations with a lot of shitty guys, but it's never hurt one of my friends. I've been a wreck about it all week.

Desmond didn't want to tell you, but I knew you'd never forgive me if I kept it from you. I know I'm only hurting myself by telling you this, but I had to do it for you. I'll understand if you don't forgive me."

I can't believe this. That doesn't sound like Desmond. "Was *he* drunk?"

Tonya's jaw drops, and she stares at Violet for a moment, then stands and marches off to the other side of the room, her back to Violet. "Was *he* drunk..." she spits angrily, then spins back around like a fury. "Because if *he* was drunk, then I guess that makes it okay, right? Really, Violet? *Really?* I mean, I expected you to be mad at me. It's only human. But to excuse *him?* That, I didn't expect. Don't you think more of yourself than that? Is that the kind of man you want to be with?" In the course of her speech, Tonya has gone from anger to hurt to concern. The emotions change so quickly that Violet hardly knows what to make of them.

"I'm sorry," she finds herself saying. *This doesn't make sense. I don't understand.* "No, that's not the kind of man I want."

"Violet," Tonya strides over and kneels at her side, her hands on Violet's, "I know this is hard for you, and sometimes when this kind of thing happens we just want to forget, to close our eyes and pretend nothing has happened, but I can't let you do that. Fuck, it would be easier for me if you did! But I care too much about you to let that happen. He slept with me, when I was drunk. I can't tell you what to do about it, but you have to face it. You have to do *something.*"

Violet hasn't moved yet, but now she stands up slowly, gently pulling her hands out from under Tonya's. The burning feeling has moved straight to her heart, which feels like it is swelling, pulsing, making its frenzied way straight up her throat, where it threatens to burst from her mouth if she doesn't do something quickly. "I'll be back," she squeaks, walking blindly toward the door.

She vaguely senses Tonya crying again behind her. She goes back to Tonya's room and gets her phone, which she carries into the bathroom, locking the door behind her. She climbs into the dry tub and sits upright, back against the hard porcelain. She rests the back of her head against the wall and presses, trying to center herself. She looks at her cell phone in her hand, and finds herself squeezing. *This didn't happen. This didn't happen.*

This didn't FUCKING happen. She raises her phone into the air to smash it against the bottom of the tub, and somehow realizes that will only make things worse. She forces herself to breath and dials Desmond's number.

The phone rings once... twice... three times... four... *Maybe it's not true. Maybe she's just screwing with me. Maybe she's joking.* Violet's hand squeezes around the phone.

"Hello?"

She is silent for a moment, trying to form the words. She has no air. She starts to cry.

"Violet? Is this you?"

"So I hear you fucked Tonya," she bites out, trying to control her voice.

"She told you. Damn it! Violet, I fucked up. It was stupid and mean and... God, Vi..." He is crying now too. "Are you at Tonya's? Can I come get you?"

Why is he crying? What the FUCK??? He sounds so vulnerable. "Why did you FUCK her?" Violet knows she is being too loud. Tonya's parents are home. She is sobbing. She needs to control herself. But it hurts sooo bad. *It hurts! I can't stand it.*

"I don't know! *Please*, Violet, let me see you. I'm an ass. I shouldn't have done it. I didn't want to tell you cause I didn't want to hurt you. It was a mistake, and I would never, EVER do anything like that again. I love you, Violet."

Stop, stop, STOP. "She says she was drunk." *Did this really happen? Is this real? Please, God, make this go away. Make it not have happened!* "Did you fuck her cause she was drunk? Cause I was away for two days? So you thought you could just get her drunk and have her on the side?"

"What?" He sounds genuinely confused, but Violet's not having it.

"That's why you always said you didn't like her... cause you wanted to FUCK her and you talked shit about her to throw me off." Violet has forgotten about Tonya's parents. She's forgotten about Tonya. She's almost forgotten about feeling hurt, so massive is her wrath.

"Vi..."

"SHUT UP, you ASShole!" she roars, then more quietly, "I don't wanna hear it. You are fucking slime. We're over."

"STOP. Violet, you can't do this," he pleads.

Desmond, do something. Make it stop. Come here. Make it not true. "You fucked up. I mean, if you guys had just fucked each other, maybe…I might have been able to get over that. But she doesn't even remember it Desmond. She was so drunk, she doesn't even know what happened."

"Oh, my God, Violet," his tone has changed. "That's not true." Then louder, "Vi, she's fucking *lying*!"

She is? "Yeah, I'm sure," she comes back sarcastically. But in her head: *tell me, Desmond. Tell me she's lying!*

"Violet, I swear," he sounds desperate again. "We were both drinking, but *I* was more drunk than *she* was! I was all fucked up, and she started crying cause some guy dissed her, and she made me hold her and she was crying…"

"STOP!" *I don't know, I don't know.* "You're not gonna blame her!"

"No, I know. I'm not trying to blame her," his words rush out, crashing against her resolve like a tidal wave. "It wasn't her fault. We both fucked up. But she wasn't that drunk, Violet, I SWEAR she wasn't. She remembers. Just give me a chance! Let me make it up to you. Let me come talk to you…"

"I don't know," she says firmly, sounding calm and resolved when in her head she's falling to pieces. "Just… not tonight. I gotta go, Desmond. I'll call you tomorrow. I gotta go." *I can't take it, I can't take it.*

"Violet, no…"

"I'll call you tomorrow." She hangs up. She looks at the shower curtain and imagines it closed around her, protecting her in a dark cocoon, but she doesn't move. Her phone rings. She shuts it off without looking at it. *This sucks.* She cries openly, big, fat *fuck my life* tears. "This SUCKS," she proclaims to the empty room. She sits there for several minutes, lost. There is nothing she can do that will make this better. There is nothing anyone can do that will make this better. She drags her heavy body out of the tub and drifts back to the game room, where Tonya is standing at the open window smoking a cigarette. It is snowing.

Tonya sees Violet walk in. She inhales deeply from the cigarette, and extends it toward Violet as she blows smoke toward the window. "Did you call him?"

Violet walks across the room to Tonya, takes the cigarette, and leans out the window with her elbows resting on the sill. She takes a drag. *This is gross.* She takes another drag. "Yeah," she responds flatly. "He said sorry."

"Pshht. I'm sure he is." Tonya picks a pack of cigarettes up off the window sill and lights one. "I got us a pack today. I thought we might need it. I've been smoking like a chimney all week." Tonya's tone is heated, but she is much more animated than Violet, whose body is no longer warm. It's no longer much of anything. She can feel the frigid outside air moving through her like a sieve. The cold bites, but it doesn't bother her.

"So how was it?" she asks without emotion.

"Huh?" Tonya takes another drag of her cigarette.

"Desmond. How was he? Did he at least make it worth your while?"

"That's a weird question." She almost sounds offended. "He didn't make me come, if that's what you wanna know."

Hmph. Violet smiles wryly. *Don't remember, huh T?* "Mmmm. Gotcha. Well, don't feel bad." *Who gives a fuck anyway?* She pulls hard on her cigarette. She's used to the taste now, and the little buzz it gives her is a good reminder that she's still here. Her soul hasn't skittered off yet.

Tonya may have realized her slip, because she adds, "I just remember bits and pieces. It's like a bad dream. Are you okay?"

Because you care so much, don't you? "Yeah," Violet replies, "I'm great. It's just a guy. There'll be others." *I guess. All bastards, but whatever.* "You got an ashtray?"

"Just put it out on the windowsill. You can't tell when the windows closed."

You're an idiot, thinks Violet, but she does it anyway. "So we gonna watch a movie?" She won't look at Tonya, but Tonya's not paying much attention anyway.

"Yeah, whatever you want. Is that what you wanna do?"

"Sure." Violet walks back to the couch and sits numbly in the corner where she sat not long ago, listening to the story of her betrayal.

"You poor thing." Tonya draws the window down and crosses to the couch. "We're gonna find you another guy *this* week."

Mhmm. That'll fix it. Violet smiles again, not a happy smile, more of an 'I hate you' smile. "Sure. Pick a movie." *I'm not gonna make this easy for her. It's not my job to make this okay. It isn't okay.*

"How bout a horror flick? Something with a lot of guys getting torn apart." She scrolls through the options.

Wow. You are really that oblivious, aren't you? Violet doesn't bother answering, she just watches Tonya. *I can't believe you are my friend.* And her eyes grow wet, in spite of herself.

It's a long night for Violet. She rockets back and forth between sadness, anger, confusion, denial, and even moments of giddiness. She never turns her phone back on, although she thinks about it often. Tonya seems to come to a point where she actually thinks that Violet's okay. Once that happens, Tonya is no longer sad or angry about last weekend. In fact, it's as if nothing has even happened. She trashes Desmond like he's some ex-boyfriend from another lifetime, and gossips about this person and that. Violet just lets her talk. *It's easier if I don't think about it.* Time ticks by... slowly. Very, very slowly. *I want to go home.* But she plays it off. She won't let Tonya see her weakness. She won't let anyone see her pain. *I hate you,* she hears herself think, many, many times. She thinks it at Tonya, at Desmond, at herself, at her mother, at her father, at life.

At 2am, Violet suggests that it's time for bed. "Oh my God," Tonya exclaims, "I'm not tired at all!"

"I am," Violet says, though she knows better. She just wants a break from Tonya. She wants to be in her own head, as scary a place as that is right now. "You staying in here?" They're still in the game room, watching television and messing around on the internet.

"Yeah, I can't sleep yet," Tonya announces casually.

No dip. "Kay. I'll see you in the morning." Violet heads to Tonya's room, where she climbs into Tonya's queen size bed and waits. *God, I just wanna sleep.* The tears come again, silently this time. She lies still, tense, her body exhausted and her mind wide awake. The thoughts change, but the tone is the same. *I can't take it. I can't handle it. This didn't happen. I don't care. I don't wanna care. I love him. It's okay. It's not okay. It hurts. It hurts. Oh my God, it fucking hurts.* She hears Tonya come in, and stays very still. *Don't talk to me. I'm asleep.* Tonya seems to drift off quickly. Violet's not sure she ever sleeps that night.

23

Violet gets out of bed at 7am Sunday morning. It doesn't hurt so bad anymore. Now it's more of a dull ache than a sharp pain. She can handle it if she doesn't move too quickly. She eases out of bed, puts her phone in the pocket of her sweatpants, opens the bedroom door, and listens carefully, not wanting to see anybody. She doesn't know if Tonya's parents are early risers because she and Tonya never get up early when she sleeps over. She can't hear anything, but it's a big house. She walks quietly down the hall to the game room. She thinks she can hear something down in the kitchen, but it's too quiet to be sure.

The coffee table in the game room is still covered in remnants of last night: nail polish remover, used paper towels, bottles of nail polish, an empty soda can, a dirty glass. It smells like smoke in here. *So much for smoking out the window. I wonder if Tonya's parents know? They probably wouldn't care anyway.* She walks toward the window, which now frames a light frosting of snow over the world. Violet looks around for the pack of cigarettes as she crosses the room, but doesn't care when she can't find it. Her mouth tastes like stale smoke already. She leans her forehead against the cold glass, but it is too much. She pulls her head back, not wanting to connect with the world. Wanting instead to hide from it.

The couch welcomes her when she lays her body down, and she imagines herself sinking right inside of it. She turns on the t.v., just to fill her head, and flips the channels absently. *I wonder when Mom can get me.* Mom doesn't ever sleep in, but that doesn't mean she's gonna want to get Violet this early. *I'll text her.* Violet pulls out her phone and turns it on, hoping for pages and pages of missed text messages from Desmond, but unwilling to acknowledge that hope. There is one unread message: i'm so sorry i hurt u. plz call me

That's it? Anger... Resentment. The hurt is boxed up well for now, so she doesn't feel it. *Wow, I can tell you feel really bad. Jerk.* She texts her mother, letting her know that she's ready to go.

Violet's out of Tonya's house before Tonya even wakes up. She spends most of Sunday at home in bed. Desmond calls once, in the middle of the day. She doesn't answer, although she hears it ringing. Her phone is right beside her in the bed. He doesn't leave a message. *Oh my God, Desmond. Don't you care about me? Are you even gonna try? You cheated on me!!! Act like you care...* But when she checks her phone again, there's still no message.

The hurt is boxed up, but the disappointment is there. Maggie knocks on her door at around 2:00. *Go away. I don't wanna see anybody.* Violet doesn't respond to the knock. Maggie opens the door and pokes her head in. "Mom said to come down for lunch," she says softly, and waits.

"I'm not hungry," Violet whispers, suddenly feeling more sad than she did a moment ago.

Maggie walks over and sits beside her on the bed. She puts a hand on Violet's shoulder. "It'll be okay," she says gently, and Violet feels that Maggie cares.

"Desmond and Tonya hooked up." Violet is lying on her side facing the door, staring straight ahead.

"Oh, my God," Maggie gasps. "Like, kissed hooked up?"

"No, like... had sex hooked up." It feels yucky saying it, and she wishes she hadn't. She flips over to lie on her other side, facing the wall. "I don't wanna talk about it. Tell Mom I'm not hungry."

"That is so fucked up." Maggie is indignant.

Well, it's none of your fucking business. Violet is suddenly mad at Maggie. She knows that Maggie hasn't done anything wrong, but she's making it worse. "Can you just get out?"

"Violet, don't let them get you down. I know it hurts, but…"

"Oh, my GOD, get OUT!!!" Violet demands. Maggie is ruining the numb feeling that has been keeping Violet safe all day. "I *said* I don't want to *talk* about it!"

Maggie's face goes all hard and she glares at Violet. "Fine," she responds, getting up to leave. "I'm sorry I tried to help."

Whatever. The door shuts behind Maggie. *Fucking people are all the same. Nobody cares about me. You just care about yourselves. Thanks for nothing, Maggie.* It takes awhile for Violet to find that numb place again.

Violet falls in and out of sleep the rest of the day, but it doesn't seem to make the time pass any faster. At 4:00, Mom knocks on the door with a plate of food. She brings it to Violet in bed, but doesn't have any words of comfort. She just says, "Eat up. You'll only make it worse if you don't eat." Violet doesn't respond, yet she eats all of her tomato soup and tuna sandwich.

At 6:00, Mom comes to the door again. The empty bowl and plate are still sitting on the bed. *Oh my God, leave me alone.* Violet rolls over and calls out, "yeah?"

Mom opens the door. "Desmond's here. Do you want to see him?"

A flicker of hope sparks in her chest. *What's wrong with you, Violet? He's a jerk. Why would you even talk to him?* "Sure." *Whatever.*

"Should I tell him to wait in the living room?" Mom is still standing in the hall with her hands holding the door.

"No, just tell him to come up." Mom gives her a skeptical look, to which Violet's face responds sarcastically, *what?!!* Mom shuts the door and Violet is alone.

It is an awkward conversation between Desmond and Violet. He wants to be forgiven, but isn't giving her any time to forgive. In his attempt to get past the discomfort, he demands that she make a choice now. Does she want him or not? For her part, Violet is angry at him for hurting her, desperate to feel better, and resigned to feel miserable no matter what she does. In the end, Violet decides to give him another chance. He cries a little when he takes her in his arms. She cries too, but the tears are different. His tears say, *I'm an ass, I'm so sorry,* and *I'm so glad you've taken me back.* Hers say, *you're an ass, I don't know why I'm doing this,* and *I will never trust you again.*

24

The whole week is shitty, made more so by the fact that last week was so great. Violet keeps to herself, sitting by herself in class and shutting herself in her room at home. Tonya was irritated when she found out Violet got back with Desmond, but she's not making a big deal about it. They're just kind of avoiding each other. Violet told Cecilia Monday morning what had happened, but they didn't talk about it. Violet has made it clear to everybody that the topic is not open for discussion. The less said, the better. She sleeps a lot, and writes some in her old journal. She hasn't written in her journal since 7th grade. The writing makes her more angry, which is okay, because angry is easier than sad. Desmond tries to see her a few times, but she makes excuses. She doesn't talk to him on the phone either, except for a couple of 2 minute conversations. She finally tells him that she has been getting headaches and needs to rest. He sounds disappointed, but doesn't argue.

On Friday at school, Cecilia sits next to her in the lunchroom, declaring companionably, "We need to talk." Today is the first day all week that Violet has come into the lunchroom to eat. She's been hiding out in hallways, stairwells, and empty classrooms.

"Okay?" Cecilia is the one person Violet can't be mean to, no matter how bad she feels.

"Not now. What are you doing tonight?"

Sleeping. "Nothing."

"Yes, you are. You're coming to my house."

"Cecilia, I haven't been feeling well…"

"Yeah, we know. You've made that quite obvious. Look, I understand how you feel…"

No, you don't.

"…but you're shutting everybody out. You got some bad news, and you're sad about it. Of course you are. Anyone would be. But you have to talk about it, cause pretending everything's just fine and normal is obviously not working. I'm your friend, and I'm not leaving you alone anymore."

Cecilia, please leave me alone. "I don't know. I'll see." Violet pokes at her pizza, but doesn't eat.

Cecilia is becoming indignant. "Vi, you just told me you're not doing anything tonight. I'm your friend and I need you. My mom can pick you up at 6:00."

Violet has to smile a little. Cecilia knows just how to work her. "You need me?"

Cecilia grins, "Yes. I need you. You've been worrying about *you* all week, and tonight you have to worry about *me.*"

Violet is still smiling, but it's a sad smile. She looks at her plate, not hungry at all. "Okay." The girls sit together until the lunch bell rings.

On the bus that afternoon, Violet and Cecilia chat pretty easily. *I need to snap out of it. I was getting sick of Desmond anyway.* But when she walks into her bedroom and sees the utter mess that it has become, the heaviness creeps back in. *I can't deal with this.* She drops her book bag on the floor, kicks off her shoes, and climbs into bed with all her clothes on. She cries a little bit before she falls asleep.

■ ■ ■

Friday night turns into something quite different from what Violet was expecting. She felt better almost as soon as she left her house this evening. Not exactly cheerful, but more like herself than she's felt all week.

Cecilia and Violet are in Cecilia's kitchen fixing ice cream sundaes when the doorbell rings. Violet looks at Cecilia. Her brother's away at college, and her mom never has visitors. Cecilia doesn't look surprised. "Don't be mad," Cecilia warns, putting the ice cream scoop down in a bowl and walking out of the kitchen.

Desmond, Violet thinks, scowling. *Just what I needed.* But it's not Desmond. Violet can't hide her surprise when she looks up to see Tonya walking in. Cecilia has made herself scarce.

"Hey," Tonya ventures, still standing near the doorway.

"Hey!" Violet replies with false levity. "Want some ice cream?" She has already turned to the counter, giving Tonya her back.

"Can I talk to you?" Tonya asks.

No. "Sure!" Violet gets another bowl out of the cabinet, and Tonya walks over and leans back against the counter so that she can see Violet's face.

"Violet, I'm sorry," Tonya states evenly, looking at her eyes.

"I know. It's fine," she responds, working the scoop slowly into the frozen block before her.

"No, it's not." Tonya is more serious, more grownup sounding, than Violet has ever heard her. "I lied when I said I didn't remember. I did remember, and I know you know that. You wouldn't have gotten back with Desmond if you didn't know that. I lied about not remembering, but I didn't lie about the rest... about how sorry I was. I was only thinking of myself that night. I was lonely and I felt rejected, and there was Desmond."

Violet is not messing with the ice cream anymore. She stands with the scoop in her hand, staring down at the countertop. No one speaks for a moment, and then Violet responds, "that sounds like Desmond."

"I know…" Tonya is still looking at Violet, defenses at rest. Her arms are crooked back, with her hands wrapped around the edge of the counter. "I don't even think he was trying to get in my pants at first. I think he was just trying to be a friend. I'm glad you're back with Desmond, Violet. I shouldn't have done what I did. I get so freaking jealous of you. I mean, I didn't plan to kiss him. I wasn't trying to do that. I think I just wanted to know what it felt like to have a good guy for once. Guys like that don't like me. And you are so strong. Nothing ever seems to bother you. I guess I let myself think that it wasn't that big a deal, but I know it was." She is crying now. "I really need you to forgive me, Violet. You're the best friend I ever had."

Violet looks at Tonya, who's not sobbing or screaming or tearing at her hair, but looking at Violet, straight in the eye. *She's not faking it.* Her own eyes fill, then her cheeks grow wet. These are not the hopeless, desperate, *I can't stand it* tears that she's been crying all week. This feels different. This feels like opening the box. Like letting go. She doesn't say anything, just lays the ice cream scoop on the counter and hugs her friend tight. "Jealous of me?" she manages. "You're crazy. Any guy would be lucky to have you." Tonya just hugs Violet tighter.

The three friends spend the rest of the evening together. They talk about their friendships, about their romances, about mistakes and moving on. It's not a sad evening, exactly, but it's poignant. They get honest with each other. Even about how annoying it is that Cecilia's always trying to bring everybody together! Over the course of the evening, Violet makes a decision. She doesn't tell her friends because it wouldn't be fair to him, but she has decided to end things with Desmond. Maybe not forever, but definitely for now. She won't ever forget what Tonya did, but she can accept it and move on. Tonya's one friend among many. With Desmond it's different. It was supposed to be just him and her, and he's ruined that. She looks forward to talking to him tomorrow. It's been a long week, and it won't be over until she talks to him. She'll call him when she gets home.

25

Rachel doesn't get home from the gym until 8:30 on Friday night. She was relieved when Violet texted earlier to say she would be sleeping at Cecilia's. Maggie told Rachel what happened with Desmond and Tonya. She is sympathetic, but it doesn't make Violet any easier to live with. *I swear, that girl thinks the world revolves around her.* Her bedroom is totally trashed, she leaves dirty dishes all over the kitchen, she's constantly snapping at Rachel and Maggie, and all she wants to do is lie around feeling sorry for herself. *You're not gonna feel better if you don't even try.* Rachel drops her keys and cell phone on the table in the front hall and retreats to the kitchen. She pours herself a glass of cranberry juice with club soda and makes herself a salad. Fresh spinach, feta cheese, cucumbers, plum tomatoes, olives, and chopped pecans. She tops it off with a Light Italian dressing, and eats standing up at the kitchen island.

She plans to catch up on some work this evening, and is reviewing her to-do list in her head when she hears her cell phone ringing in the hallway. *Oh shoot. What now?* She puts her fork down and heads out to the front hall. *Violet, please don't be calling asking to come home.* And as she picks it up, *I should let it go to voicemail.* "Hello?"

The voice on the other end of the line is tentative. "Hello?"

This is not Violet... "Matt?"

"Hey, Rachel… Did I catch you at a bad time?" No longer tentative, just polite.

"No!" *What did I sound like?* "No, this is a great time. Hi." *Why is he calling me?* She walks back to the kitchen island, where she left her food. She picks up her fork to eat, then realizes she can't eat salad and talk on the phone at the same time.

"Hi. Listen, I'm sitting here alone at the house, Renee took the kids to her mom's house for the weekend, and I just thought maybe I'd call and see if you wanted to have dinner tomorrow night. Maybe I could even pick you up, let you get a little bit tipsy. I'm guessing you don't do that much?"

Hmmm. That sounds rather pleasant. Does your wife know? "Oh, Matt, that sounds nice. I don't know, though. I mean, there would be no need for you to pick me up…" *Should I ask about Renee? I don't want to offend him.*

"Oh, I'd be happy to! Renee always drives when we go out. I remember you complaining that you were always the designated driver. Let me do this for you. I'm bored. I need something to do this weekend."

Okay, I was kidding when I said that about being the designated driver. But he's talking about Renee, so she must be fine with it. Why not let myself be spoiled one night? "Okay, it's a deal. Shall I text you my address?"

"Sounds good. 8 o'clock okay?"

"That works for me!" *Sorry, girls. I'm going out tomorrow.* "Where shall we go?"

"Hmmm. What do you like? Steak? Italian? Mexican?"

"I'd say Mexican or Italian. Or French? Have you been to Le Catedral?"

"Nope, but that sounds good. Tomorrow at eight?"

"See you then!" Rachel hangs up. *Nice. Okay, what's next?* She resumes her mental to-do list as she finishes her dinner.

26

Saturday morning, Violet, Cecilia, and Tonya make plans for that night. Some guy from Everbrook High is throwing a party, and they're gonna go. Cam said he would drive them. Violet can't help but have flashbacks of Desmond taking Tonya to a party, but she doesn't say anything. Anyway, it's not like Cam and Tonya are going without Cecilia. Violet wonders what Cecilia would say if that were the case. She wonders if *she* should have said something before the New Year's Eve party, like told Desmond not to take Tonya. *That's stupid. I can't control what two people do when I'm not around.* She lets it go. The girls try to convince Violet to invite Desmond. She insists that she needs a night out without him, yet finds herself questioning her resolve to break up with him. She decides she won't make a final decision until she has some time to herself.

At home that afternoon, Violet is disappointed to find herself feeling down again. It's not the intense gloom and dread that have been weighing so heavy on her; it's more a vague sense of unease, of dissatisfaction. Maggie and Mom are practically ignoring her, which just makes it worse. *What is their problem? Whatever. I'm going out tonight, and I'm gonna have fun! Screw Desmond. Screw Mom and Maggie.* An image of her dad pops into her head, but there is no narrative to go with it. She pushes it quickly back out again.

Violet spends some time straightening her room, but doesn't make much progress. It's too messy and she's too distracted. As she aims to clear off the top of her desk, she recalls the secret admirer notes still buried within it. She pulls them out, thinking all the while of Desmond. The text was her favorite. The 'you're awesome and super hot' one. *That's right, I am. Too bad you forgot that for a minute, huh D?* The third one kind of annoys her. *Still waiting patiently? Well, where the heck have you been for the past month? Are you gonna be at the party tonight? Hmmm. Screw it!* She decides to call Desmond. It's time.

■ ■ ■

Rachel is feeling good this evening. She had Maggie fix her hair so it's nice and smooth and shiny. She's outlined her eyes in a deep brown liner that makes them really pop. She stands in front of her bedroom mirror in her bra and panties, looking at her muscles as she turns this way and that. *Not bad, Lady. Not bad at all.* She puts on the black mini dress and silver spike heels that she got for a trip to New York a few years ago and checks herself out. *Oh, no. Much too much.* She didn't wear it in New York, either. She tries on a lavendar sweater next, but feels like a schoolgirl in it. *I'm not twelve.* After a couple more tries, she finally settles on an above the knee, loose black skirt, a gray fitted cardigan, a pink silk tank that gathers at the collar bone, and plain black pumps. Pearl earrings and a pearl bracelet finish off the look. It's 7:50. Maggie has already gone out for the evening with some girlfriends. Last time Rachel saw Violet, she was putzing around the kitchen, but she has plans to go out this evening as well.

■ ■ ■

Violet sits by herself at the kitchen island eating a Weight Watchers pasta dinner. She has never understood why Mom buys Weight Watchers. Nobody in this house needs to lose any weight, but whatever, it's easy and it tastes good. Violet usually eats two or three before she feels full. She'll pop a second one in the microwave while she gobbles down the first.

Mom doesn't know about that, which is why she jumps when she hears her coming down the stairs. *Where's the box?!! Gotta hide the evidence... oh, phew.* Tonight she's only fixed one, so she's good.

Mom is going out to dinner with some guy from school. He should be here any minute. *It's... 8:02. That's Mom! Always rushed, but never late.* Violet invited everybody over at 8:30 to hang out before the party. Mom doesn't know about that either. "Wow," Violet says when Mom walks in. "I thought you said you were going out to dinner with a *boy* from school. What kind of *boy* is this?" Mom looks really good tonight... *for Mom, that is.*

Mom fixes herself a glass of water, not paying Violet much attention. "He's a young, married man with children, who sees me as a mentor. Life is about more than just romance and parties, Violet. You need to learn that."

Mentor? Pffft. Okay, Ma, mentor away! This guy really must have problems if he wants you for a mentor. Violet doesn't say anything at first, just looks at the clock, hoping her mother will be leaving any second, then it strikes her: "Why is he taking you out to dinner?"

"Don't talk with food in your mouth. He's not taking me out to dinner. We're going out to dinner together, because that's what adults do. It's called networking. You'll need to learn about that if you're going to be a performer. It's not what you know, it's who you know."

"Mmmm. So if you're the mentor, what's in it for you?"

Mom rinses her water glass and puts it in the dishwasher. "Run this before you go out tonight." She crosses the kitchen, "and wipe off the counter after you eat. I'm going to check my email." The doorbell rings. "Whoops. See! That's an accountant. Always on time." Mom smiles as she walks out.

Wow, nerd fest of the century. Wish I were going out with you guys! God... Violet picks up her disposable dinner plate and non-disposable fork. She swipes the counter with her hand to clean it, drops the plate in the trash can under the sink, and tosses the fork into the utensil bin in the dishwasher. She has taken a shower and dried her hair for the party, but she still needs to get dressed and everything. She heads upstairs. The conversation with

Desmond earlier went okay. She didn't tell him she wanted to break-up. Instead, she just asked him if they could take a break. He didn't really say anything, so apparently it wasn't that big a deal. *Maybe he's been waiting for me to break up with him. Maybe when things were bad, it was cause he really just isn't into me anymore, and then he was nice to me last week cause he felt guilty. Well, don't be with me cause you feel guilty! You're not that special, Desmond Jones.*

Violet starts to put on her favorite pair of jeans, but pauses with one leg in and one leg out. *New me! Let's see...* She drops her jeans to the floor and heads to the closet, sliding her clothes across the rack bunch by bunch. *Nothing...nothing...nothing.* Back to the dresser. She opens the top drawer. *Underwear, underwear, bra, bra, underwear. Next?* She pushes it closed and moves on down the line. *T-shirt, long sleeve, tank, shorts.* Next drawer. *Jeans, sweats, paper, shorts. Shoot.* One more drawer. *T-shirt, sweater, skirt?* She pulls it out and holds it to her waste. It's light blue with painted looking flowers. *Eew.* She throws it on top of the clothes in the drawer and pushes it halfway closed with her foot. *Jeans, it is.*

As Violet pulls her jeans back on, a new idea occurs to her. She smiles to herself. *New me?* She opens her top drawer. *Just for tonight.* She pulls out the pushup bra that she bought with Tonya last Fall. She doesn't need it, but... *hehehe. See what you're missing Desmond?* She bought it a size too small for emphasis, and it definitely does the job. Violet works to keep her thoughts facing forward as she finishes putting her *look at me* outfit together, complete with a low cut, skin tight shirt. All day, she has been feeling a tension in her stomach, especially since she talked to Desmond, and it's getting worse. It's like she's nervous or something, but she doesn't know why. *How can I be nervous? Nothing's going on at school. Nothing's going on at home. I'm taking a break from Desmond, which I think I'm actually happy about. Is it Tonya?* She waits for her body to tell her. *No, it's not Tonya.* Whatever it is, it doesn't feel good. It's making her increasingly restless and uncomfortable. *I wonder what Mom has to drink downstairs.* Mom is not a regular drinker, but she usually has wine in the house. If there's an open bottle, Violet might be able to get away with drinking a little. If nothing's opened, forget about it. Mom doesn't drink beer or liquor, but sometimes there's some leftover from a party. Violet finishes getting ready and heads downstairs to see if she can find something to take the edge off before her friends get here.

■ ■ ■

Le Catedral is a mid-sized restaurant with super high ceilings, painted black over exposed industrial metal beams. The restaurant is kept fairly dim, and there are different colored spotlights aimed disparately across the ceiling, creating an effect reminiscent of traditional stained glass, but with an abstract, contemporary twist. The theme is carried throughout the décor with traditional white tablecloths under square, black plastic placemats, ornate draperies adorned by huge raw wood cornices, and intricately carved candles set atop large squares of smooth, colored glass. There's background music that seems to be French, but it's so quiet it's barely audible. Rachel started with a cocktail, then Matt had her choose a bottle of wine to share. True to his word, he is drinking very little. Rachel has just finished her second glass when the cheese plate arrives, after salad and entrees. She had the poached salmon and he had the duck confit, which he devoured.

Matt starts to pour her a third glass. "Oh, my goodness," she protests, "I don't think I can handle anymore. *You* have a glass. You've only had one."

He finishes filling her glass, then fills his own. "I'm driving, remember? There would be no point in me driving if you were planning to go home totally sober."

Rachel is feeling a little giddy. She obediently sips her wine. "Good point. A toast?" She raises her glass toward him, and he raises his as well. "To new friendships."

Matt taps his glass against hers. "To new friendships."

Rachel slices a piece of brie and takes a bite, letting it melt between the tip of her tongue and the roof of her mouth, then slide smoothly back down her throat. *I need to stop eating. This is ridiculous.* She puts another bite in her mouth. *But so good.* "So, since you and I are getting to know each other so well, I'd love to have you and Renee over for dinner sometime."

He looks at her quizzically. "Uh, right." He sort of chuckles, "we'll have to see if we can do that sometime. You ready to go back to school?" Judging by the way he attacks the cheese plate, that duck must not have been as filling as it looked.

"Oh, yes!" Rachel responds enthusiastically. "It gives me an excuse to pull my head out of taxes for a few minutes a week. I don't know how I'll handle tax season without it!"

Matt has his elbows on the table and is smiling at her appreciatively. "It's really hard for you to just let go, isn't it?"

Rachel sips her wine. She feels her insides growing warmer, and she laughs at the irony. "I was about to say no, but I guess that boat sailed when I described graduate school as my form of relaxation, huh?" *Am I too uptight? No, I don't think so. Just responsible. Mmmm, this wine is delicious.* The third glass is going down as smoothly as the brie.

"Well, I hope you feel like you can let go tonight. Are your kids home?"

"Nope! Both girls are sleeping out tonight. One's got a party, and the other one went to the movies. How often does Renee go away with the kids?"

"Oh, maybe once every two or three months. I bet it's hard for you to relax when the kids are home. This must be a rare opportunity for you to just let go."

"Oh, no. They go out all the time. Teenage girls, you know?" *Wow, I'm really talking a lot. I should be quiet.* "They're always either out with friends or have friends over. The only issue is having to drive them around, but one already has her license and the other will soon, so I'm almost home free!" *Slow down with the wine, Rachel. Oh wait… why should I? This is my night, right?* Matt hasn't said anything, so Rachel keeps talking. "I mean, not that they're a burden. Well, the younger one can be. She has been driving me crazy all week. Boy trouble. She acts like it's the end of the world!" *Why is he looking at me like that?* "So, what about you?"

"Huh?" Matt looks confused.

"How are your kids? Do they drive you crazy?"

"Oh, no. They're great. Did I tell you how pretty you look tonight? I mean, not as a come on, but you do. You look really stunning."

Awww. She can feel herself blushing, and looks away from him. "You look very nice also." *Okay, change of subject.* "So, what are you doing your thesis on?" *Oh, did I finish my wine already?*

"I gotta be honest, Rachel. School is the last thing I want to talk about right now. How about you tell me about… your next vacation. Where are you going on your next vacation? And you look like you need some more wine…"

■ ■ ■

The party at Ryan's house is re-freaking-diculous. Violet didn't think she knew Ryan, but she recognizes him from the coffee shop when he lets them in. She didn't wind up drinking anything at home and that strange, nervous feeling is still in her stomach, so she goes straight to the 'bar' when they get there. It's actually a table with bottles of vodka, rum, and tequila, a big tub of canned soda and ice, and a keg on the floor next to it. Ryan is charging a $3 entry fee to cover his costs.

Violet is standing at the bar trying to figure out what to do with this mess when some guy she's never seen before walks up next to her. "You look like you could use some help. Coke or orange?"

Huh? She doesn't answer, trying to translate what he just said into something intelligible. She just gives him a confused look.

"Just trust me. Which do you like better?" He grabs a big plastic cup off the table.

"Orange?"

"Sweet." He hands her one of the cups. "Will you get me a beer while I hook you up?" Without waiting for an answer, he opens a bottle of vodka and begins to pour.

Violet is trying to figure out how to use the keg when Cecilia and Cam walk over. "Like this," Cam says, doing it for her.

"Oh, thanks." She takes the cup of beer and trades it for her vodka and orange soda. The guy is looking at Violet, so she takes a sip. He looks all excited. "Good," she tells him.

"Cool," he nods, then "cheers!" to Violet and her friends. He wanders off.

"Who was that?" Cecilia asks.

"*What* is that?" Cam asks.

"I don't know," says Violet to Cecilia, taking another sip, "and vodka with orange soda. Here," she holds her cup out to Cam, "it's not bad."

"That's okay," Cam does not look impressed. "Don't go too crazy with that vodka. You know you can't taste it," he warns, getting himself and Cecilia each a beer.

Violet ignores him. She wasn't really meant to respond. Cecilia gets her beer from Cam and the three move out from in front of the bar to survey the scene. It's really crowded, and the air is thick with cigarette and marijuana smoke. It doesn't look like that many people are smoking, but still. There's pop and hip hop music playing at full blast, but Violet can't tell where it's coming from. Probably just an Ipod speaker system or something. A short, skinny blonde girl grabs a tequila bottle off the bar, takes a swig, and passes it to the girl next to her. She sees Violet watching her. "Shots!" she calls out.

"Cheers!" Violet responds, holding up her glass. *Freaky much?* She turns slightly away from the girl so as not to encourage further conversation. "So," she yells casually. She has to shout to be heard over the people and the music. "Desmond and I are taking a break."

"What?!!" Cecilia's jaw drops. Cam takes a sip of his beer and averts his eyes.

"Caaam?" Violet questions him. She knew what Cecilia's reaction would be, so she's more interested in what Cam has to say.

"Nothing," he responds innocently.

"I thought…" Cecilia starts. "Oh, shit, it's too loud in here. Let's go outside."

"I don't wanna talk about it." *If I wanted to talk about it, I would have told you two hours ago at my house.* "Let's just have fun. Right, Cam?"

"Cam," Cecilia interrupts, "tell her to come talk to us!"

Cam doesn't move. "Vi, I like Desmond. He's a cool dude. But he did you wrong. I think you did the right thing."

"Thank you," Violet smiles, disregarding Cecilia's dumbfounded expression.

"Fine," Cecilia acquiesces, "we'll have fun. Hmph!" She folds her arms in mock irritation.

"Cecilia," Cam wraps one arm around her shoulder, "is this your way of telling me you wanna screw my best friend?"

"Shutup," she laughs, slapping his chest. "Come on, let's see who we know here." Cecilia, Violet, and Cam begin to work their way through the crowd.

■ ■ ■

When it comes time to pay the tab, Rachel has to fight to get Matt to split the bill. He wants to cover all of it, but she's not going to let that happen. It's not that she doesn't believe in chivalry, because she does. She's always telling the girls to let their dates pay when they go out. She just doesn't like the idea of being in anyone's debt, and this is a friendship, not a date. Matt finally agrees to split the bill if he can cover the bottle of wine, but she doesn't bow easily. "Matt, it's ridiculous for you to pay for the wine when I drank most of it!"

"Rachel, I'm a man taking a woman out to dinner. Do you know how embarrassing it is for me to have people see you pull your wallet out? Just let me pay for the wine, for the sake of my pride."

"No deal. We split the bill, 50/50." She is trying to drive a hard bargain, but it's hard when her head is spinning.

"Okay. How about this: Remember that expensive bottle of French brandy you were bragging about? The one you've been savoring forever because it's so precious? Let me pay for the wine, and you can cover your debt by fixing me an after dinner drink when I drop you off at home. Does that sound fair?"

Having you in my living room sounds more than fair... Oh, stop, Rachel! Lord, I drank too much. "Yes," Rachel resolves to sober up between now and then, "that sounds fair."

"Thank you! Let's pay the bill and I'll get our coats."

■ ■ ■

Violet has finished her first drink and moved on to a second. She doesn't realize it, but the drink she fixed herself is much weaker than the one she had earlier. That first cup was probably 40% vodka, and it loosened her up very quickly. It's the first time all day that she feels comfortable in her own skin. That nagging discomfort in her stomach has been anesthetized by alcohol.

The large living room is packed with people, some dancing, some sitting, and some just standing around. It's hot and sweaty, but nobody cares. Cecilia and Cam have gone off to make out in a corner somewhere. Violet and Tonya are dancing with a group of guys who might have partaken in those tequila shots that were making their way around earlier. The empty bottle has long since disappeared. It's not just Violet and Cecilia that are dancing with these guys. Everyone is just kind of dancing with each other, rocking, rubbing, bumping, and turning. One of the guys holds a joint up to Violet, but she shakes her head. *I don't even want this cup anymore.* She's beginning to realize how drunk she is, and is feeling reminded of the crazy, scary nights she and Tonya have spent getting messed up together. *Uggh, let's not go there.*

Violet turns away to find a spot to put her drink down, and a different guy grabs her arm. He's tall, brunette, with long arms and wide shoulders. He has smooth skin and chiseled features. This is the guy that Violet's had her eye on. "Hey," he calls to her, "don't go!"

She laughs, "I'm not going! I'm just done with this drink." She sidles back closer to him.

He looks in her cup. "You're not done with it! Come on, drink up!"

"Nah. You want it?"

"Sure!" He knocks it back in two gulps, drops the cup on the floor, and puts his hands on Violet's waist.

Uh, oh. She instinctively looks around, thinking of Desmond. *Oh, wait, there is no Desmond.* She puts her arms around the guy's neck, moving with him to the thump of the bass. Tonya is nowhere to be seen. *She must have gone to smoke. No worries. This is getting interesting.* Desmond is quickly forgotten.

■ ■ ■

We're here already? Rachel watches Matt walk around the front of the car to open her door. *That was a quick ride.* She hardly even remembers getting in the car. Her decision to sober up during the ride home hasn't proven as easy as planned. All the lights in and around the house are off. It is a dark night, with no moon and hardly any stars. Rachel is glad she let Matt be the driver. It would have been disappointing coming home alone to this dark, cold night after such a nice dinner. He opens the car door and leans in to help her up.

"Oh!" Rachel exclaims softly when he puts his left arm around her back and gently takes hold of her right arm with his other hand. She doesn't mean to, but she lets herself lean into him as they walk up the front path.

"It's cold," he says, holding her close.

"I know," she replies evenly. "It will be warm inside." It's hard to get her key out of her purse without putting space between them, and she doesn't want space between them. She may never be this close to him again. She brings her purse around in front of her body and presses her elbows against her sides as she works her fingers around to find the keys. Instead of loosening his hold, he pulls her in closer. *Is this okay?*

When they get through the front door, Rachel steps pointedly out of his arms and leads him into the living room. "Have a seat. I'll get the brandy." *Should I have put him in the kitchen? Is the living room too comfortable? Am I giving him the wrong impression?* She makes her way to the dining room, where she keeps her liquor and brandy snifters in a sideboard. *Oh, this is silly. He was just being polite… and flirtacious? So what, it's just flirting. He's happily married. You're not a prude, Rachel. Relax a little.* She fixes two small snifters of brandy. *I really don't need any more alcohol. Just a taste to be polite.* She pours more into Matt's glass so as not to seem stingy.

Back in the living room, Matt has settled himself into the brown armchair by the television. *Good. Not too close.* Rachel hands him his glass and sits on the couch across from him. As soon as she sits down, he gets off the chair and comes to sit down next to her, about an arm's length away, as evidenced by the arm he has draped across the back of the couch. *Okay. This is okay. I guess.*

He sniffs his brandy before taking a sip. "Wow, I can see why you've been hanging on to this. It's delicious." He has another taste.

Rachel is watching him drink as she holds her snifter to her nose. She touches the golden liquid to her lips, letting just a trickle into her mouth. It doesn't burn like the cheap stuff, but creates a gentle warmth, like being wrapped in a down comforter. She thinks about kissing him. She thinks about him kissing her. She tries to tell herself to stop, but she can't focus long enough. Being with Matt is like being in a storybook. He doesn't belong to work or home, to family or to her normal circle of friends. *He's married, Rachel.* She breaks from her reverie and puts her glass down. Before she even realizes what is happening, his glass is sitting on the table next to hers, his arms are wrapped around her, and his lips are brushing her neck.

■ ■ ■

Violet hasn't figured out this guy's name yet, but she's not worried about it. She isn't out to find a new boyfriend. She just wants to dance and have fun, to feel beautiful and powerful and excited. She can feel the stress of the past week falling off her shoulders like chunks of snow piled too high on the tree limbs. For the past twenty minutes, it has been just Violet and him. Violet doesn't know where her friends are, and she doesn't care. Tonight is about Violet. No one else matters. She presses her body against him, laughing and teasing with her caresses. She feels... joyful... perhaps even free. Not a care in this big, bad world. She is dancing and she is beautiful and the world is at her feet.

■ ■ ■

At first, Rachel just lets him kiss her. Her eyes are closed and her head is tilted to the side. It is even better than she imagined. She doesn't even touch him at first, but then her hands move to his chest. He is firm, muscular. His heart is racing, and so is hers. *Rachel, stop.* But she doesn't. She turns her head to meet his lips. She feels her body go soft, and she finds herself pulling at his shirt where it is tucked into his pants. *No. Don't. You can't.* But she does. He is pulling her sweater off her shoulder, kissing her gently wherever he finds skin. He has started on the buttons of her sweater.

Rachel manages to pull away from him, swooning as she stands up. It takes a minute for her to get her bearings, and by the time she has, he is at her side. His lips are on her ear, his right hand has come up under her blouse, and his left is on her bottom, inching her skirt up with his finger-tips. *It feels so good. I shouldn't. But it feels so good. I don't care.* She let's go, and he feels it. He whispers in her ear, "where?"

"Upstairs." She can't look at him. *My God Rachel, what's wrong with you?* She takes his hand and pulls him behind her, up the stairs and into her bedroom. He pushes the door closed and takes her by the waste, guiding her to the wall next to the door. He presses against her, running his hands up her thighs, under her skirt. *Don't think, Rachel, don't think.* He is taking her clothes off now. *He's married! What is wrong with you?!!* But she cannot tell him to stop. Her body will not let her.

■ ■ ■

Violet is really sweating now. She's so hot and she's been dancing so long that she can barely breathe. Her guy friend seems to notice her slowing down. He pulls her into his chest. "Hey!" she laughs, pushing him away. "I can barely breathe as it is. I think I need off this dance floor!"

"Me too," he steps back, taking her by the hand. "Come on." He pulls her toward the living room doorway.

Yes! Fresh air. She follows willingly. "Your shirt is soaking!" She runs a hand playfully down his back. "I don't think there's a dry spot on it."

He turns back toward her and wraps one arm around her waste, put-ting his other hand on her stomach as they press through the crowd. "I don't think yours does either, but I'm willing to do some more research."

"Gross!" Violet laughs, pushing his hands away. "Where's the door?" It's so dark and smoky and crowded, Violet can't see clearly where they're going.

"Right here," he elbows past a couple sucking face in the hallway, and pulls Violet into the bathroom.

Bathroom? Eew! "I am not going to watch you pee, if that's what you're thinking." She grins at him broadly.

He laughs, "Whatever." He puts an arm around her waist, a hand behind her head, and smashes his lips against hers. His breath smells like cigarettes and alcohol.

Gross! She raises both hands and pushes against his chest, but her back is against the wall and she can't get much leverage. *This is nasty! Drunk bastard can't even kiss.* She manages to turn her face away, and he is kissing her cheek and her neck. "Stop," she says firmly, but he doesn't. She pushes harder, but it doesn't seem to make a difference. "STOP!" she commands. He doesn't respond. *Oh, shit.* She realizes something is not right here.

He takes his arm off her waist and presses his whole body flat against hers. He is holding her head in both hands now and forcing his tongue into her mouth. She presses her lips together as hard as she can, but his tongue still makes it inside. *Oh my God, GET OFF!* She can't even talk now. His tongue is gagging her. Her heart races. He lets the pressure off with his body. *Thank God!* She pulls her head back and starts to stand up, but he wraps an arm around her head so that she can't turn it either way, and he leans into her hard again. *Oh, my God... I don't know what to do!!!* His tongue is still in her mouth, moving around like a fat, muscular worm, and she can't move her head. *GET OFF!!! GET OFF!!!* His other hand is pulling her shirt down at the neck, reaching in her bra. His hand is on her bare breast.

She begins to throw her body side to side wildly, striking with her shoulders and scratching with her nails. *I can't get him off!!!* Now he has her shirt and bra off her shoulder and halfway down her right arm. He grabs a handful of hair at the nape of her neck and holds it tight. He uses his other hand to hold her right arm against the wall. His lips are on her nipple. She pounds and grabs and scratches at his head with her free hand, growling at him, pleading, "PLEASE, stop! Please, please STOP!" She is too embarrassed to yell, and too scared to cry. *I can't be seen like this. I need help. Please don't let anybody see this!* He bends to get his mouth under her breast, and she manages to throw her hip to the side, get her right leg under her, and slam her left knee into his rib cage.

"Whoa!" He stumbles back, laughing. "Calm down!"

What?!! She is stunned for a fraction of a second. "YOU ASSHOLE!" she screams, pushing him back with both hands. She tears out of the bathroom, pulling her clothes over her breasts as she goes. She moves down the hallway as fast as she can, angry tears streaming down her face. She has a vague sense of people staring at her as she pushes her way out, but she doesn't take the time to notice who or where or why.

Violet is on the front steps now, then jogging out toward the street. She is crying for real. *Aaaaah, what is WRONG with people!* She wants to tear at her skin, pull out her hair, rip her breasts off, wash her mouth out with bleach. *What the FUCK is WRONG with people?!!* She slows her pace, walking quickly down the side of the road now. Her heart is still pounding. *I have to calm down.* She slows her pace further, trying to gain control, slowing her breathing. *Where are my friends?* She feels so sad and alone. *I need my freaking friends.* She stops at the corner, her head in her hands, tears flowing like river rapids. She knows she has friends here, but she doesn't want to go back. *Fucking Asshole.* She rubs her arms, trying to make herself feel safe again. *I hate this. God, why did this happen to me? I don't understand!!!* She stands alone on the corner for several minutes, pacing, calming herself down. *I need to go home. I'll be okay. It's okay. I just need to go home.* She gets her phone out of her back pocket and sends Cecilia a text: we hav 2 go. It's not long before Cecilia gets her out of there.

■ ■ ■

Rachel wakes up to a hand on her arm, shaking her steadily. Her eyes snap open. *Matt?* She remembers. *Oh, no.* She closes her eyes. Her head hurts, her lips are swollen, and her mouth is dry and stale.

"I should go," he murmurs, and kisses her on the cheek before he climbs out of bed.

Rachel nods without opening her eyes, then lies still, listening to him dress. *What time is it?* She doesn't move until he says goodbye and shuts the bedroom door. She looks at the clock: 5am. *I can't believe I did that.* She climbs out of bed and puts her robe on. *I need to lock up.* She walks down the stairs and runs into Matt, just opening the front door.

"Hey," he turns back to her. "That was amazing, Rachel."

Amazing? She can't believe her ears. "No, Matt," she responds coldly. "That was terrible. Please go." Her arms are crossed, and she feels vulnerable standing there in nothing but a bathrobe.

"Oh, Rachel." He takes a step toward her, then stops, sensing her anger. "Neither of us ever meant for that to happen. And I know it was awful. I feel terrible for doing it. But it happened. There's nothing we can do to change that, and I'd be lying if I tried to say that being with you was anything less than incredible. I know I can't have you. I've made my bed; that ship has sailed. But let's not regret our one night together."

You slimy son of a bitch. You egotistical, self-centered bastard. "Get out, Matt." She sounds like Rachel now. Tough, powerful, dominant, in control. "And don't call me again."

He drops his head and his shoulders, as if abashed. "I'm sorry," he says, turning and walking slowly out the door.

Whatever. You're full of crap, and I'm an idiot. I should never have crossed that line. God, you screwed up, Rachel. What were you thinking? She shuts the door and locks it behind him. *The lights.* It's a dark night, and she hasn't turned on the outside lights. *Oh, screw him. Let him trip.* She walks back upstairs to shower off her sin.

27

Violet is tired, but not sad today. There's been too much sadness already. She got back from Tonya's a couple of hours ago, and has just finished journaling about what happened last night. Someone once told her that when you go through something tough, it's not healthy to keep it stuffed inside. You need to get it out. This time, that tactic seems to be working. When they left the party last night, she didn't tell anyone what had happened right away, but she didn't pretend nothing had happened either. The plan was to sleep at Tonya's house, which they did, and Violet asked Tonya to give them some space so she could talk to Cecilia alone. She may tell Tonya about it at some point, when it's not so fresh, but Tonya's not allowed too close to her heart right now. *I love her, but she's right. She's not as strong as I am, and I can't pretend that she is. What happened last night isn't gossip or drama; it's my life. I'm not gonna let Tonya turn this into another one of her soap operas.*

When they got to Tonya's house, Violet showered, brushed her teeth, brushed her hair, and fixed herself a hot cup of tea before she was ready to tell Cecilia about the assault. A year ago, Violet would have been too ashamed to tell her. Tonya maybe, but not Cecilia. She would have blamed herself for leading him on and for not sensing sooner that something was wrong. She is not that person any longer. *I'm not perfect, I might have sent some mixed signals, but no way did I deserve that.*

Violet closes her journal and secures it in the desk drawer. She doesn't even realize she's laid it on top of her secret admirer mementos. When she woke up this morning at Tonya's, she had a bowl of cereal, but she's hungry again. She goes down to the kitchen to see what they have, and when she gets there, Mom is eating a sandwich at the kitchen table. She's got her laptop open in front of her and a mess of papers spread out all around her. "Where's Maggie?" Violet asks.

Mom doesn't look up from her work. She looks harried. "She went out with your father."

"She did?" *Why didn't he take me?* "Where did they go?" Violet hasn't seen much of her dad lately. She feels a little hurt.

"Believe it or not, I think he actually took her to look at cars. She called me this morning and said he's been doing some research, and he wanted to take her out today." Click, click, click. Her fingers move swiftly over the keyboard.

"Oh." *What about me? He hasn't even called me in, like, two weeks.* "Cool." *I hope he buys her a car. She needs him to do something like that for her.* Violet sits across from Mom at the table. "Watcha eatin?"

Mom stops typing and looks at Violet. "Bologna and mayo. Would you like to fix yourself one?"

"Maybe." Violet studies her mom. *She looks tired.* "How was last night?" Violet puts some pep in her tone, attempting to brighten Mom's mood.

"Fine." Mom starts typing again. She takes a bite of her sandwich, wipes her fingers on a napkin, then jots something on one of her papers.

Violet is feeling strangely drawn to her mother today. Maggie is out with Dad. Violet is recovering from a very draining couple of weeks. Mom is solid, never moving, never thrown off course. *Mom works so hard. Maybe I'm too hard on her,* she thinks, as she watches Mom toil. She is struck by the urge to open up to her, pull her closer. "So, the party was kinda crazy last night."

"Mmmm." Mom's not paying attention, focused on her work.

Violet gets up and walks to the refrigerator. "You want a drink?" She grabs bread, jelly, and peanut butter to make herself a sandwich.

"Hmmm. How about a cup of coffee?" Mom is still distracted, typing away. They have one of those one cup, instant coffee makers in the kitchen, so it's not a big deal to fix a cup of coffee.

"Kay. Lemme just make my sandwich." Violet gets to work on the bread. "Yeah, so, you had a good time at the restaurant? What did you eat?"

Mom finally seems to get the hint. She pushes her laptop toward the middle of the table and stands up, turning toward Violet. "Poached salmon. It's a nice restaurant." Mom gets herself a coffee mug and makes her way to the coffee machine.

"I'll do it!" Violet protests as she slices her sandwich in half.

"It's okay," Mom says without emotion. "So, the party was fun?"

"It was okay," Violet replies. She drops her knife in the sink and fixes herself a glass of milk. "Actually," she carries her lunch to the table and sits down, "there was a lot of drinking going on." *Not that that's unusual, but you don't know that.* Violet is testing the waters, trying to see how far she can go. *It would be really nice to tell Mom about the guy in the bathroom.* She feels guilty when she sees Mom put the bread, jelly, and peanut butter back in the fridge. *I was gonna put it away in a minute.*

Mom pours cream into her coffee and sits down across from Violet. "Drinking, huh? I hope *you* weren't drinking."

Should I tell her? Violet looks into Mom's hard face and decides to go a little further. *She was young once too.* She tries to make herself look regretful. "Actually, I had one drink." *I mean, if I never drank, it would have been like I* did *have only one... big one.*

"Violet, you know better! I mean, come on. It's not like you haven't seen what alcohol can do to a person." Mom's tone is harsh, but Violet can tell she's more irritated than angry.

Note to Self, don't ever tell Mom about all the times you've gotten drunk and high. Violet still wants to connect with her. She doesn't want to fight with her. She sticks with her plan of attack: "Trust me, I know. Some drunk guy tried to kiss me." She wills her to sympathize: *Come on, Mom... act concerned.* She waits with baited breath, looking at Mom's face.

"What? Well, what were *you* doing?" Mom still sounds harsh.

"We were just dancing and stuff, and next thing I know his hands are all over me and he's trying to stick his tongue down my throat." She says it as if it were no big deal, but she feels a little sick when the words cross her lips. She doesn't want to show her vulnerability, not knowing if Mom will be sympathetic or not, but she hopes Mom will read between the lines. Violet stares into her lap. *Say something nice, Mom. Please, don't be a bitch right now.*

Mom's face has changed, from concern to contempt. She lies both hands flat on the table in front of her. "So you were drunk, dancing with some strange guy, and then he tried to kiss you. Do you even know his name?"

Oh, shit. That was not the point of this conversation. Why did I open my mouth? "I wasn't drunk, I had one drink. Forget it. I didn't kiss him. He tried to kiss me, and I told him to screw off."

"Oh, that sounds pretty. I'm glad that's how my daughter talks when she's out in public. And do you think that maybe the way you were dancing had anything to do with his decision to kiss you?" Rachel can't help but think about her own detestable behavior last night.

What the fuck? Violet is not letting Mom's reaction hurt her, but she's beginning to feel offended. And she is definitely regretting bringing this topic up. "I was dancing, Mom. I wasn't stripping for him. Just forget it, okay?"

"So you tell me a boy tried to stick his tongue down your throat, and I'm just supposed to forget it? Why would you even tell me that, Violet? I mean, is that something you feel proud of? You seduced some poor boy and then got him so enamored you had to fight him off? Are you just telling me that to get me upset? Why did you tell me that?" She is enraged with her daughter.

Holy shit. Mom is practically shaking. Is she crying? "I'm sorry, Mom." *Jesus Christ, she's freaking lost it.* "It's fine. It was nothing. I'm sorry."

"Well, next time think before you speak." Mom pulls her laptop back towards her on the table and starts typing violently, but Violet suspects she's mostly pressing random keys.

Violet picks up her plate and cup and goes to sit down in the living room. *Goddamn, I thought I had problems. She's out of her freaking mind.* It's the first time Violet has ever looked at her mother and seen anything other than strength. It's almost comforting, to think that Mom is not so abnormally sane as she has always seemed. Maybe there's some human in there after all. Violet finishes her lunch, contemplating recent events. *People really are freaking crazy. Desmond and Tonya fuck each other, and they're both crying for me to forgive them. Some random guy tries to rape me at a party, and Mom is blaming me for it. My God, maybe I'm not the crazy one after all. Might need to find some new people to hang out with, but at least I haven't lost my freaking mind.*

She lies down on the couch, folds her hands behind her head, and lets her eyes rove over the ceiling. *At least I have Cecilia. And Maggie. She's not the best sister ever, but she's not mentally disturbed.* Violet does a mental review of the healthy people in her life, from different friends to aunts and uncles to teachers. It is comforting to remind herself that there are good people in her world, in spite of all the crazy ones. *I wonder what ever happened to that secret admirer? I wonder what his deal was?* She lets herself smile as her imagination takes over, envisioning one ludicrous scenario after another to explain her dear, crazy stalker boy. *He's like my teenage imaginary friend,* she giggles to herself. She remembers that she actually had an imaginary friend in preschool, and she would scold her sister and parents for sitting on him at the table. *Wow, I was ridiculous,* she thinks without judgment, and she drifts off unexpectedly into a heavy, dreamless slumber.

SPRING

28

Over the next several weeks, Violet finds herself in a constant state of assessment. She ponders the quality of her relationships and interactions. She imagines herself an expert at reading people, like on her favorite tv show, *The Mentalist*. She studies the people around her and tries to predict their actions even before they know themselves what they're going to do. It gives her a sense of control that she really needs right now. She turns her emotions off and just watches, cold and detached.

Two weeks before Spring semester midterms, Mom is going on a long weekend to the beach with some girlfriends, and Maggie is riding with Grammy and Grandpa to visit Uncle Ronnie, so Violet is spending both Friday and Saturday night at Dad's. One night at Dad's is rare; she probably hasn't spent a whole weekend at Dad's since she was around eight-years-old. She could have found a friend's house to stay at, but she just never bothered to make the arrangements. It's 8 o'clock on Friday, and she and Dad have just gotten back from dinner. She watched him knock back three rum and cokes while they ate, and now he's just opened up a beer to drink while they watch a movie together. Donna has been conspicuously absent all afternoon.

Violet looks in the pantry for some microwave popcorn, which is one of those items that Dad always seems to have and Mom never does. She has begun to lose patience with her father. It's true that he doesn't mistreat her, but isn't being a drunk a form of mistreatment in itself? And where is Donna? It's not unusual for her to be out when Dad is home, but normally he would say something about it. He hasn't mentioned Donna once today. Violet keeps her tone casual, despite the doubt in her mind. "Where's Donna?" *Please don't say you've screwed it up, Dad.* Donna has been around for a long time now, through jobs and joblessness, sober stretches, drunken binges, religious crazes, she's always been there. It occurs to Violet as she waits for Dad's response that she has learned to count on Donna to keep him safe. *You need her.*

"Violet, you drink with your friends, don't you?" He is standing behind Violet, near the kitchen table.

She turns to face him, popcorn box in hand. "Sometimes."

"How would you like to have a beer with me?" he asks seriously.

Mom would kill you. I don't know if I want to have a beer with you. You shouldn't be offering me a beer. I'm your daughter. I'm sixteen. "Sure." She is doing it for him, to make him feel comfortable. *He doesn't want to drink alone.* Violet can imagine that this would be a real bonding moment for some people, but not for them. This doesn't feel like bonding; it feels stupid and unnatural.

He gets another beer out of the fridge, pops the top, and hands it to her with an awkward smile. "You're the best daughter a man could ask for." His eyes are moist. "I love you Violet."

This is awkward. "I love you too, Dad." She takes a sip. "So?"

"So?" He looks confused. The sentimental feeling seems to have passed.

Violet looks at him steadily, beer in one hand, popcorn in the other. "Where's Donna?"

He sighs loudly. "I think I fucked up, Violet." His voice is ever so slightly slurred.

Violet is taken aback. *Don't talk to me like that, Dad.* She's not used to him cursing so openly in front of her. Not in conversation with her, at least. Maybe when he's drinking with his friends. She puts her beer down on the kitchen table, then puts the popcorn down as an afterthought. "What'd you do?" she asks. She doesn't really want to know; she asks because she's supposed to. *I don't like this.*

He takes a gulp of his beer, then another. "She told me not to buy that car for Maggie. I mean, she wanted me to, but when I had saved up." He is silent for several beats. "I took the money out of our savings to buy it. Not really our savings – her savings, but she had my name on the account in case there was ever an emergency."

Oh shit. Violet doesn't know what to say. Dad bought Maggie a car weeks ago. He had been talking about it forever. *Why is this all of a sudden a problem now?* Dad seems to read her thoughts.

"I told her I bought it with my money. She went to take out money for Mike's tuition, and it wasn't there. I thought I could put the money back before she noticed. She's really mad at me, Vi." He looks at the beer in his hand, takes several swallows all at once, and stands the empty bottle on the table. "I don't know how to make this right."

Violet's first instinct is to feel sorry for him. He looks so pathetic, as helpless as a child. He sighs again, shakes his head, and goes to the cabinet. *He's going for the liquor.* Violet watches him, observing him as if from afar. *You're not a child, Dad.* She thinks about Donna, who is nothing like Mom. Donna is patient, supportive, accepting, loving even. Violet could always see Dad's side when she listened to Mom complain about him, but Donna? What has Donna ever done but take care of him? *I don't think I've ever heard Donna complain or ask you for anything.*

He pulls a bottle of whiskey out of the cabinet, but it is almost empty. He looks at the bottle, looks at her, shrugs and opens it. "I wouldn't normally do this, but no reason to waste a glass for one sip." He drinks, smacks his lips, drinks again until it's gone.

"I don't think you should do that, Dad." Violet never questions Dad about his drinking. That's what Mom and Maggie do, not her. But what did that get Donna? *Damnit.*

Dad nods his head in agreement. "Probably not." He caps the empty bottle and carries it over to the sink, where it will sit on the counter until someone takes recycling out. "Another beer?" he offers.

Wow. Violet is not angry, but she isn't sympathetic either. *How do I respond to this? I love him, but he shouldn't have done that.* "I love you, Dad."

She says it sincerely, but without passion, her body watchful and alert, still deciding on the next move.

He tilts his head and smiles at her from under his eyebrows.

Don't go all mushy on me, Dad. It wasn't that kind of I love you. When he hugs her, she wraps her arms around his shoulders and hugs him back firmly. This is an important hug, because she has just realized something. *I can't do this anymore.* This was supposed to be a normal weekend. Maybe boring and maybe fun, but not particularly memorable. Something about hearing what Dad did to Donna has changed that. Maybe taking the money wasn't anything epic. Maybe it was just a small error in judgment, but it was one mistake too many. She puts her hands on Dad's shoulders and steps away from him. "You need to fix this, Dad. Donna was the best thing you ever had." She drops her hands. "You should call your sponsor," and she turns and walks away from him. Violet has no idea whether Dad has anybody he calls a sponsor these days or not, but she knows he'll get the message. He created a problem, he needs to fix it, and until he does, he's on his own. *I'm done holding your hand, Dad*, she thinks as she retreats upstairs to the guest bedroom. *Time to man up. Let me know when you get there.*

If she listened, Violet would hear Dad messing around in the kitchen and living room for several hours, but she's not listening. She'll spend the night here tonight. *No big deal.* She has her cell phone, her Ipod, and a book to read. But tomorrow she'll stay somewhere else. At Cecilia's or Tonya's... there are lots of people she can call. She won't tell Mom about tonight, but she may have to tell Maggie if Dad and Donna don't work things out. *Poor Maggie. She won't know what to make of this. She'll blame herself cause Dad bought her the car, and it's not her fault. Donna wouldn't blame her at all. I'll tell her before Dad does, cause he'll only make it worse.* Violet has a flash of anger when she imagines that Dad might try to get Maggie to sell the car, but it passes quickly. *I won' let her.*

Violet makes herself at home on the second floor of the townhouse. She's not avoiding Dad, but she suspects he may be avoiding her. She takes a shower, sends out some texts, secures a bed at Sarah's for tomorrow, sits by the window listening to music and picking out constellations, and finally snuggles into bed. She has just begun the paperback mystery that she brought with her. She's got over 400 pages of entertainment to guide her into sleep. Violet asks herself repeatedly if she should go down and talk things over with Dad, but she comes back to the same answer every time, and she really feels okay about it. *I love him. I told him I love him. That's all I need to do.*

29

The following Saturday, Violet and Tonya go to the mall to pick out a birthday present for Cecilia. They've already made plans with Cam and a couple of other people to surprise her at La Fiesta Mexican Restaurant tonight. She'll be seventeen on Monday. The mall is pretty empty for 3:00 on a Saturday. The weather has started to warm up as Easter approaches, and today is a particularly pretty day. The sun is shining brightly, puffs of white clouds dot the sky, and the air is warm in the sun with a gentle breeze that makes it just right. Violet is anxious to get their shopping done and get out of the confines of the mall.

The girls have been browsing for a couple of hours. Tonya bought herself a pair of jeans on sale and two overpriced tank tops that just got put on display. Violet picked up a short sleeved shirt on clearance for $4.00, but they haven't found anything that looks right for Cecilia yet, and they've already hit all their favorite spots. "Should we go in Macy's?" Violet wonders. The girls are ambling down the main corridor, looking for inspiration.

"I guess. What can we get her besides clothes? There's nothing good here." Tonya is bored.

"She likes clothes," Violet counters. "Let's just keep looking." Cecilia is the only one of the three that worked a paid job last summer, at McDonald's. She would still be working now, but her mom won't let her when school's in. Tonya always has money; she just has to ask her parents and they hand it over. Violet's parental dividend is more sporadic, but she gets money when she needs it. Violet volunteered at Theater in the Park last summer, which was cool because Desmond always had money anyway. This summer will be more complicated. Cecilia is pretty much on her own for anything beyond the basics, just because her mom can't afford a lot of extras. *We're gonna find her something good.*

"Okay, let's go to Macy's," Tonya agrees. "But we're gonna get her something there. We need to stop just looking at sale stuff." She picks up her pace, ready to take care of business.

"Fine, but you're paying for my dinner if I spend all my money on Cecilia's present." Violet quickens her step as well.

"Just ask your mom for more money!" Tonya says it like it's so obvious, but both girls know that she'll cover Violet's meal if she has to. Violet doesn't bother to reply. Tonya will never understand what life is like for kids whose parents don't say yes to everything.

The girls are able to find a whole outfit for Cecilia: shorts, shirt, and a necklace that Tonya just had to get her. She'll keep the matching earrings for herself, because "I don't want her to feel like we spent too much on her." They sit on one of the metal benches outside the mall, waiting for their rides. Tonya's getting picked up by Marcus, and Maggie's coming for Violet. Tonya was supposed to ride with Maggie too, but Violet didn't care when she asked if she could call Marcus instead. "I just wanna spend some time with him, you know?" *Yeah, I know. No biggie.*

So Violet is sitting on the bench listening to Tonya describe how amazing Marcus has been, how "he's changed" and "I think I'm in love with him." Tonya's face is expressive: smiling, then gazing soulfully off into the distance, scowling, then spreading her arms to embrace the wonder of it all.

Violet watches Tonya, observing the utter self absorption of her monologue. It's that cardboard feeling again. They've been sitting out here for twenty minutes, with Violet providing the backdrop to Tonya's amazing life story. It just isn't very satisfying. In the past, Violet has either stayed in character, playing the good listener, or tried to compete with a tale of her own. The competition is a joke. Tonya will win every time, if only because she could care less what Violet has to say. And staying in character is just... boring. So she considers her options: *Tell her to shutup? Nah, too harsh. Get up and walk away? Nah, too cold. And that will just start a fight.* "Tonya," Violet interrupts her. "I don't really care about Marcus." She says it nicely. Not irritated. Not judgmental. Just the fact: I don't care. Then she winks at Tonya companionably.

Tonya is looking at her, mouth open in mid-sentence. "Oh." She's lost for words.

"But I love you," Violet smiles. It feels good to just say what she thinks. A lot of times, she puts other people first, and that feels good. That's what friends do. Lately, she's learned what it feels like to put herself first. She's learned to look somebody right in the eye and say: it's my turn now. And she doesn't feel a bit bad about it. *I deserve some happiness too, and I sure as hell can't depend on anyone else to give it to me.*

Tonya looks irritated, but she doesn't say anything.

"Sorry, Tonya. It's just, a couple months ago you were telling me you broke up with Marcus because he was a total drug addict, and now all of a sudden he's your knight in shining armor." Violet is watching Tonya's face as she talks, using it to guide her words. "If you guys last, then I'll care about Marcus, but for now, how bout we talk about something else?" Slowly, Tonya's face softens, like she realizes this is okay; this doesn't have to be a fight. "What are you doing for Spring break?" Violet probes. And just like that, they are chatting again.

30

Maggie stops and stares at Violet, who is standing at the stove stirring a large pot of marinara sauce. Every countertop in the kitchen seems to be strewn with dirty dishes and culinary garbage, but Violet doesn't care. She's making Grammy's pasta sauce, and it's worth all this mess. *Go away, Maggie. Let me work.* She keeps stirring.

Maggie shakes her head and walks out of the kitchen. She's just gotten home from somewhere or other. She's out a lot now that she has her own car.

Violet puts her wooden spoon down on the counter next to the stove and starts gathering dishes to pile in the sink. It's just the cutting board, knife, and vegetable peeler. She puts the can opener by the sink too. It's splattered all over with tomato juice. She's just beginning to pick up trash when Maggie walks back in and starts straightening silently.

"You don't have to do that," Violet says, wary of her sister's reappearance.

"You're cooking; I'll clean up," Maggie insists. "Smells good."

Violet continues to clean, though not as thoroughly as Maggie. *What is she being so nice for?*

"Go ahead and put the pasta water on, if it's time," Maggie suggests. "You suck at housekeeping anyway." She's kidding, but Violet's still apprehensive. "Seriously, let me clean."

Violet stops what she's doing and gets a pot out for the spaghetti. "So, how's the car?"

"Freaking awesome," Maggie declares. "Of course, what Dad didn't think about when he got it for me is how I'm gonna pay for gas and insurance, but I was saving up for that anyway. I'm just glad I got that job at the grocery store before he got me the car. It would have sucked if Mom got stuck covering those bills. I wanna get more hours now, though."

"You want some juice?" Violet asks as she pulls a glass down from the cabinet.

"Sure."

"I guess I need to get a job soon too." *Damn, I really don't wanna work.*

"It's definitely nice having your own money. You have a lot going on at school, though. Mom's more concerned with you doing well there." She says it gently, without malice. "If I were you I would just concentrate on getting a job this summer and trying to save up so you have some cash next year."

Violet tries not to smile. *Good answer!* "Yeah, I guess."

Maggie is making quick progress cleaning up the kitchen. "So, do you know anything about what happened with Dad and Donna?"

Violet can't recall a time in her life when she knew something about the family that Maggie didn't. If anything, it's usually the other way around. Violet is surprised to find that she doesn't like being the one with the information. "Ummm, I'm not sure." She turns her back on Maggie to check the pasta water.

"You know, he had just gotten me my car when they split. He didn't say anything when you spent that weekend with him?"

She knows I know something... I think. "No." Violet's pitch is just a little too high, and she avoids meeting Maggie's eyes.

Maggie scrubs the countertop where the stewed tomato cans left sticky red rings. "They'll be okay. They always are." Scrub, scrub, scrub. "Are you?"

"Yeah," Violet declares, surprised that Maggie has noticed she isn't. She thought she was putting up a pretty good front. The truth is that underneath her happy façade, there is a place in Violet where fear and loneliness curl up together, turning their backs to the world in eternal hope that if they are not seen, they will cease to exist.

"You miss Desmond?" Maggie has finished with the counters and turns to tackle the dirty dishes in the sink.

"Actually, we just started talking again. As friends, I mean. But I didn't really miss him anyway." Things with Desmond have been different since the day Violet asked if they could take a break. They talked for about a week after that. She even told him about the sexual assault, and he was all concerned about it. He wanted Violet to help him find the guy so he could beat him up, but Violet didn't want that. Talking about that night is one thing, but she still hopes she'll never see him again. Telling Desmond was okay, but it also reminded her how much he hurt her when he cheated with Tonya. At the end of that week, she told him she wanted to break up for good. He didn't take that so well. He disappeared for awhile. She would call and text him, but he just didn't answer. Then a couple of weeks ago, she ran into him at the coffee shop. She was sitting with some of her friends from chorus, and he came over to say hello. That's when they started talking again. "I'm totally good!" *Most of the time.*

"Good. I always liked Desmond, but what he did was really shitty. You deserve better than that. I'm glad you and Tonya worked it out, though. What she did was just as screwed up, but I don't think she meant to hurt you. She really looks up to you."

"Yeah," Violet replies without feeling. *You're a worse sucker for Tonya than I am.* "How's it going with Michael?"

"Okay. I don't know how much longer we'll last, though. He's been getting a little pushy about having sex."

As far as Violet knows, Maggie is pretty strict about keeping her legs closed and shirt buttoned, even though she always keeps her boyfriends for a long time. She admires her for it, even though she can't relate. Violet couldn't imagine being with somebody that long and not getting physical, even if they didn't have sex. "Have you thought about doing it?"

"No," Maggie replies firmly. "When I have sex, it's going to be something special. I'm not even out of high school. I'm not having sex yet. If that's what he needs, there are plenty of other girls who can give it to him.

I'll find somebody else. And if you're having sex, you better be safe about it." She puts the last dirty dish into the strainer to dry. "Water's boiling."

Violet hops up from her seat at the kitchen island. *Shoot!* But it has just started to boil. She takes off the lid and throws some salt in the water before pouring the dry pasta in. "Almost ready."

"Kay. I'm gonna go see if Mom wants any."

"Kay." Maggie leaves the kitchen, and Violet finishes her work.

31

"So, what did you think?!!" Cecilia has just run up behind Violet at her locker. Cecilia's birthday dinner was not only fun, it came with a little extra surprise. Cam invited one of his friends to try and hook him up with Violet. Vi had seen him before, but never hung out with him.

Violet closes her locker and turns to walk with Cecilia to first period. "He's hot, but I don't know about dating him." He was nice, but pretty boring.

"He likes you." Cecilia's all excited.

Oh yeah, it's her birthday today. "Happy Birthday!"

"I got my appointment scheduled at the DMV. Driver's license!" Cecilia exclaims. "But tell me, seriously, what did you think?"

"I think it was fun to sit next to a hot guy on Saturday," she puts her nose in the air haughtily, "but I'm looking for more than just a pretty face."

"Uggh, fine. I know, he *is* kind of boring. I couldn't really tell Cam that, though. Okay, actually I did tell Cam that, but whatever." The girls take their usual seats in the second row, toward the center. "Do you ever miss Desmond? You guys were so close."

Why is everybody so obsessed with Desmond??? "Not like that. We've been talking lately, though. It's good to talk to him again."

"You know, I used to think you were crazy for being so serious with somebody in high school, but I kind of get it now. I mean, it's not like I couldn't live without Cam or anything, but lately it's gotten hard for me to imagine life without him. I don't know," Cecilia shrugs, "relationships are crazy, aren't they?"

"Yeah, I guess. Cam's a good guy, though. I mean, Desmond is too, but I don't think Cam could ever do anything like Desmond did to me." Even as Violet talks, she has to ask herself whether that's true. *Would Cam do that? I never thought Desmond would... but he was always more conservative than Cam. Like, more sheltered. Cam has more street smarts than Desmond. He can see through people like Tonya. Nah, Cam wouldn't do that... I hope.*

"I hope so," Cecilia responds easily, echoing Violet's thought. She had been looking vulnerable for a second, but she's good now.

The girls have gotten their books out and secured their bags under their chairs. Violet is still thinking about Cam and Cecilia when the teacher interrupts her thoughts.

"Violet." Mrs. Morrow is standing at her desk at the front of the classroom, one hand on a stack of books and the other holding something at waste level. Violet looks up, and Mrs. Morrow extends an envelope toward her. "This was on my desk. If it's not school related, please put it away."

Huh. Violet walks to the front of the classroom and takes the plain white envelope from her teacher. Her full name is written across the front in pen, and the envelope has been sealed shut. This doesn't look like an official letter.

"What is it?" Cecilia looks concerned as Violet sits back down next to her, but Violet is beginning to think this could be something fun.

Violet sticks her finger in the corner of the envelope and slides it across the top to break the seal. Inside is a typed note:

> I know I went away for a minute,
> Felt like a lifetime and a day, didn' it?
> You're single now, I'll be right there!
> Just need a day or two to make it fair.
> ~S.A. :)

Haha. Yay! Violet grins widely and makes sure Mrs. Morrow isn't looking before she passes the note to Cecilia. Almost immediately, she can see Cecilia scribbling on a piece of notebook paper out of the corner of her eye.

Who is it?!!, Cecilia writes, turning her paper so Violet can read.

Violet shrugs her shoulders and shakes her head, then writes on her own paper. *He's funny. Who would leave a note on the teacher's desk?* She is about to turn her paper for Cecilia to see when she notices Mrs. Morrow eyeing her. *Ooops.* She folds her hands obediently in her lap, trying to suppress a smile. Mrs. Morrow begins her lesson. *He better be hot!!!,* she adds, before showing Cecilia what she has written.

Cecilia just nods and smiles, looking around the classroom for a suspicious face. Nothing. When Mrs. Morrow turns her back again, Cecilia wiggles two fingers at Violet in front of her chest and mouths, *one or two days.*

Shutup, Violet mouths back, smiling and shaking her head. *Bye bye, teenage imaginary friend,* she thinks without remorse. *We couldn't last forever. Hope the real you doesn't suck.* Violet has to giggle when she finds herself sitting up a little straighter. *You're an idiot, Violet.* But it feels good.

32

Violet is excited when she sees Desmond's car pull up after school. This is the first time they've hung out in so long, and they dated for over a year. There was a time when she even thought he was "the one," that he could be her husband some day. Now, seeing him is just like putting on an old, worn out t-shirt. She wouldn't wear it to go out, has plenty of other shirts she likes better, but it's comfortable and it feels good.

When Violet climbs into the car next to him, he leans in to kiss her on the cheek and puts his hand over hers where she has laid it on the console. "I've missed you," he says as he sits back, his hand still on hers.

She pulls her hand out, squeezes the top of his hand affectionately, and guards both her hands in her lap. "I've missed you too," she says, but in a much more casual tone than he has taken.

"Park?" he asks as he pulls away from the school.

"Sure," Violet affirms. They chat easily as they ride together, like old times. In fact, in some ways, it's better than old times. When she used to talk to Desmond, it was because she needed to. She needed him to make things alright. She needed him to tell her that her thoughts and feelings were important. Now, she's not that concerned about what he thinks. She tells him because she wants to, not because she needs to.

"Damn, Vi. I hope they work it out." Desmond is responding to Violet's news that Dad took money from Donna. Dad called Violet up last

Sunday to let her know that Donna was back home, but Violet's not clear yet on how things will turn out in the long run. She didn't say anything to Maggie. Hopefully, there'll never be any need for Maggie to know.

"Yeah. What I really hope is that Dad just gets his damn life together. I think he's back going to meetings. I don't know if he'll ever really get it, though." Violet is thinking out loud. "I guess what I really want is for Donna and Dad to both be safe and happy. If being together is what makes them happy, then that's what I want. But I don't know." She stops her mouth, needing to work things out mentally before she says any more. *People are scared of change, aren't they? Is that why Donna has been with Dad all these years? Is it because she loves him, or because it has always been too hard to leave?* It's a yucky thought, and Violet is glad when Desmond speaks up.

"I want you to be safe and happy too, Violet."

She notices that he has already passed the turn for the park. *What is he doing?* "Where are you going?" she says aloud, looking around curiously.

"Oh, shoot," he turns his head from side to side, clearly unaware of the path he has taken. Instead of trying to turn back toward the park, he turns right onto a side street and parks at the curb. He turns the ignition off and drops the keys into one of the cupholders. He sits still for a moment, staring through the windshield, then turns his body towards hers. "Violet," he begins, his left arm resting on the steering wheel, and his right hand holding the headrest behind her, "when you broke up with me, I know I didn't deal with it right. I said we could be friends, but I wasn't a friend. I want to be your friend now, and no matter what you say, I will be a friend. I'm not gonna turn my back on you, but I really want you back." He looks at her hopefully. "Will you please come back to me?"

There's a heaviness in Violet's heart, and she almost wishes she could turn her feelings for him back on. She looks inside herself. Maybe there's still something there, some flicker of connection that just needs to be coddled back to life... but no, there's nothing. Sympathy, but not attraction. It's gone. *Poor Desmond. He really is sorry.* She feels sad for him. "I'm sorry, D." She doesn't know how to say it. *I just don't feel it anymore. I'm sorry, D.* "I'm sorry."

She can see the wet sheen forming in his eyes, but he turns his face away before it becomes anything more. "It's okay. It's my fault." He repositions himself to drive and turns the car back on. "Okay, friend. To the park?"

Phew. She smiles at him appreciatively. He's not going to push it. *We're gonna be okay.* "To the park," she agrees, and they proceed on their way.

33

It takes more than one or two days. Violet is climbing onto the bus to go home after school on Friday when somebody jostles her from behind, trying to rush her up the steps. She doesn't say anything, but she leans back inconspicuously and lets her bookbag bang into the person, hoping she'll knock them off balance. *Jerk*.

She forgets about it as soon as she hits the aisle, and prances to the back of the bus. *It's Friday!* She's going out with Sarah tonight. They've been getting closer lately. She's a lot of fun, and she's the only single person Violet has to hang out with these days. Violet sits in the last row next to Cecilia, who was one of the first ones on the bus today. Megan is sitting on Cecilia's other side. Moses climbs into the seat next to her, and she glares at him from the corner of her eye. *Did you push me on the stairs?* But then she forgets again.

"I brought you something," Moses says to her.

Violet looks at Cecilia, then at Moses. She's gone to school with him for years, but he hangs out in a different crowd. "Me?" she asks doubtfully.

"You." His voice is deeper than she remembers, and he's taller than her.

Didn't he used to be really short? "Okay…" She's not sure how she's supposed to respond.

"Close your eyes and hold your hand out." He's kind of smirking at her as he reaches into his pocket.

"No," Violet states, smirking back at him. He has sandy brown hair that kind of falls over his eyes. *He's still not very tall. Maybe an inch taller than me? He used to be really chubby, but that's not chub under there, is it?* She holds out her hand expectantly as she examines his face. *He has a cute smile.*

"Well, damn. You were supposed to do it! Okay," he looks embarrassed, "it's not actually a thing."

Violet still has her hand out, and is looking at him pointedly. *He has pretty eyes... light brown with golden flecks. Is he blushing?*

He has pulled a pen out of his pocket. He takes her hand and holds the pen up as if to write on it, then stops. "This is really corny. It's me," he shrugs. He looks at her briefly, then writes on her hand anyway: *S.A. :)* He drops his hands into his lap and watches for her reaction.

Moses?!! She laughs at him, and then feels embarrassed. Now he's definitely blushing. *That's so sweet... Moses.* "That's not corny... It's cute" she says, looking at her hand. She makes eye contact so he'll know she's being serious. Moses has gone to school with Violet since seventh grade. He was always shy and quiet. He hangs around with Jack and Todd; Violet talks to *them* more than Moses.

"I know you don't really know me..." he starts.

Oh my God, he is so blushing...

He looks into her eyes, and she feels her heart go pitter pat... "but I'd like to get to know you better."

Violet can't keep from smiling, and she realizes she may be blushing too. "But you weren't in the play!"

He looks confused for just a second. "Oh, the cough drops and the card? I'm always around after school. I help out with the sound for the shows."

Moses??? "You know, I think I've actually seen you hanging out with Sarah after school." *Wait a second...* "So, where did you disappear to for so long? I missed my... notes." It feels weird saying "secret admirer" to her secret admirer.

"Ummm…" his face seems to have returned to its normal color, but he still has that smile, "maybe we should get to know each other first, then talk about that."

It takes her a minute, then she gasps, appropriately scandalized. "You had a girlfriend! Hmph! We didn't even know each other and you were already cheating on me!"

He laughs, clearly more comfortable now that they've gotten past the initial awkwardness. "Well, I never stopped liking you, but it seemed a little creepy even to me to wait around for somebody who literally didn't even know my name. And I wasn't gonna send secret admirer notes to one girl when I was dating somebody else. But now… you *are* single, right?"

Violet can see the doubt flash across his face. *He has a nice face.* "Yes, I'm single," she assures him. She can't stop looking at his eyes. *Moses… hmmm.* She leans back against the seat, still smiling broadly, and decides to let him carry on, savoring the moment one second at a time. The sun is shining brightly through the dingy bus windows, creating a glare that virtually erases the passing scenery, but Violet's not concerned about that. *This could get very interesting…*

APPENDIX: TEXTING TRANSLATIONS

ik = I know

idk = I don't know

c = see

u = you

r = are

ur = you're or your

lol = laugh out loud

plz = please

omg = oh my God

lmfao = laughing my fucking ass off

■ ■ ■

Made in the USA
Charleston, SC
02 September 2016